The Missing
Championship Ring

The Missing Championship Ring

A Southside Sluggers Baseball Mystery

Created by Glenn Lewis and Gail Tuchman
Written by Daniel A. Greenberg
Illustrated by Bert Dodson

LITTLE SIMON
Published by Simon & Schuster
New York ◆ London ◆ Toronto ◆ Sydney ◆ Tokyo ◆ Singapore

LITTLE SIMON
Simon & Schuster Building, Rockefeller Center, 1230 Avenue of the
Americas, New York, New York 10020 Text copyright © 1992 by
Glenn Lewis and Gail Tuchman. Illustrations copyright © 1992 by
Bert Dodson. All rights reserved including the right of reproduction in
whole or in part in any form.
LITTLE SIMON and colophon are trademarks of Simon & Schuster.
Designed by Lucille Chomowicz.
The text of this book is set in Stempel Garamond.
The illustrations were done in black ink.
Also available in a SIMON & SCHUSTER BOOKS FOR YOUNG READERS hardcover
edition. Series conceived and text produced by Book Smart Inc.
Manufactured in the United States of America.
10 9 8 7 6 5 4 3 2 1   (pbk) 10 9 8 7 6 5 4 3 2 1
ISBN: 0-671-72929-2   ISBN: 0-671-72933-0 (pbk)

Contents

The Missing
Championship Ring

1 The Birthday Present

Andy West knocked the dust off his cleats and stepped into the batter's box. He glared out at the pitcher with a look of cool confidence.

The situation was tense. Everyone in the stadium was at the edge of their seat. The television cameras zoomed in for a tight close-up. The whole Championship Series of the semipro league was riding on this one pitch.

The pitcher wound up and fired. As the ball came speeding in, Andy cocked his bat way back, then unleashed his mighty swing. When bat met ball there was a tremendous CRACK!!

"Andy, snap out of it!" Zach Langlin yelled, as he watched Andy's big swing miss the ball by a mile. "What do you think this is, some sort of Championship Series? Relax! It's only batting practice."

1

"Sorry," Andy said, with a sheepish grin. "Pitch me another one like that, would you, Zach?"

"Okay," Zach said, his blue eyes gleaming with mischief. "But lighten up a little, Andy. The wind from your swing almost knocked me over."

When he wasn't joking around, Zach "The Tongue" Langlin was the Southside Sluggers' number-one pitcher. He was also one of Andy West's best friends.

The next pitch came in right over the plate. This time Andy didn't pretend he was in the Championship Series. He didn't pretend anything. He was just himself—Andy "Windmill" West, fifth-grader, catcher for the Southside Sluggers, and one player in the Lotus Pines Youth Baseball League who always swung for the fences.

Whoosh! The result was exactly the same. Andy took a huge swing and missed mightily.

"Please! Hurry up and hit one!" Seth Bradigan called to Andy from left field. "I've been waiting out here all day!"

Seth "Clear Out" Bradigan was the team's power hitter and an excellent fielder. In fact, he was probably the Sluggers' best overall player. His nickname came from his habit of yelling "Clear out!" when fly balls were hit anywhere near his position—even if other players were closer. Lately, he'd been trying to keep his "clear out" ways under control.

Seth and Andy had become good friends. Yet Seth still enjoyed giving Andy friendly little digs now and then.

Andy stepped back up to the plate. He gripped the bat so tight his knuckles looked like they were popping.

"Get ready to run," Andy called to Seth. "This one's going over your head!"

Once again the pitch came straight in over the plate. Once again Andy swung with all his might. And once again he missed by a mile.

"Thanks!" Seth laughed. "I wasn't ready to run yet."

Andy shook his head and forced a smile. He knew Seth was just trying to make him feel better about missing.

"Okay, that's it," Coach Terwilliger cried from the bench. "Two laps around the field, everyone!"

Andy put down the bat and started to run along with the rest of the team. When he passed the bench the coach stopped him for a moment.

"You're swinging too hard, Andy," he said gently. "You just have to meet the ball. Make contact. You don't need to hit it out of the park every time."

"I know," Andy said, hanging his head and rubbing his curly black hair. "I'll try to remember, Coach."

The coach had told him the same thing all season. It was good advice. Cut down on your swing. Make contact. But for some reason, when Andy came up to the plate he always ended up taking monster windmill swings.

Andy ran off to catch up with right-fielder Rachel Langlin, Zach's sister, near the foul pole.

"Hey, Rach," he said, shifting his husky shoulders. "Which do you think I am: a *power* hitter or a *singles* hitter?"

"I don't know," Rachel said, her red braids flicking up and down as she jogged along. "Which would you rather be?"

"What's that got to do with it?" Andy asked.

"Everything," Rachel said. "It's your birthday. You're the birthday kid. That means you can be whatever you want today."

"Aw, give me a break," Andy said. "I'm serious about this. I'm worried about my hitting."

"Don't worry," Rachel said. "Just take it easy like everybody has been telling you."

Suddenly Zach, who was cruising along at the head of the pack on his long, slender legs, called out. "Hey, Andy! What's your mom doing over there?"

Andy looked past the backstop to the picnic table area. His mother was placing a large green-and-orange shape on one of the tables.

"It's a cake!" second baseman Luis Diaz called out.

"An ice-cream cake!" Zach Langlin cried.

"How can you tell it's an ice-cream cake from all the way back here?" center fielder Susan Stein asked.

"H.P.," Zach said, pointing to the small, tan, shaggy-haired dog jumping up and down near the table. "He loves ice cream."

H.P. was short for "Home Plate," the Langlins' dog and newly named Sluggers mascot. Whenever food was around, H.P. was sure to be close by.

"Hey, Coach," Zach asked. "Is practice officially over yet?"

The coach nodded. A minute later the whole team had gathered around Mrs. West and the cake. The cake came in a box that said "Southside Ice Cream Shop" on it. The Southside Ice Cream Shop was owned by Ralph Langlin, Rachel and Zach's father. He was also the sponsor of the Southside Sluggers.

The cake had eleven candles on it with two plastic baseball figures on top—a pitcher and a catcher. It was green and orange to match the Southside Sluggers team colors. Almost everyone thought they were hideous colors. But Mr. Langlin liked them because they matched his favorite ice-cream flavors.

"What flavors *are* these?" Susan asked Zach, pointing to the colorful cake.

Zach took a close look. "I'd say Mint-Jalapeño Swirl and Jack-o'-lantern Fudge," he said.

"Sounds yucky," Susan said.

"My dad's ice cream always *sounds* yucky," Zach said. "But it tastes terrific."

After everything was in place, Mrs. West lit the candles, and the team sang "Happy Birthday."

"This is embarrassing," Andy said.

"Make a wish!" everyone cried, as he blew out the candles.

Zach held his fist out like a microphone under Andy's chin.

"We're here with Southside Sluggers catcher Andy West," Zach said, his voice mimicking a television interviewer. "How does it feel to be eleven, Andy?"

"Okay," Andy shrugged.

"Would you care to share the birthday wish you just made with our viewers?" Zach asked.

"As a matter of fact," Andy said, "it's not a wish. It's more like something we've got to do. Let's beat those Mudsharks tomorrow."

"Yeah!" all the Sluggers cried.

The Mudsharks were the Southside Sluggers' arch-rivals. The previous season the Sluggers had edged the Mudsharks twice to stay out of the league's cellar. But the Sluggers and Mudsharks were both getting better and their games were really heating up.

This year, the Sluggers' new coach, Coach Terwilliger, had started to turn the team around. He was helping the players improve their skills. He also helped the Sluggers play with more teamwork. Of course, having newcomer Seth Bradigan in left field had helped a whole lot too.

"Those Mudsharks really burn me up," Rachel said.

"I know," Seth replied.

"Whenever they beat us," Rachel said, "they rub it in afterward. Pointing fingers. Calling us names. Laughing. Stuff like that. Especially Chip Hoover, Billy Butler, and Big Joe Jones. They think they're so-o-o funny."

"Only one thing to do with clowns like that," Seth said. "Give 'em some of their own medicine. See how they like it."

"I don't know," said Andy, who tended to take a kinder approach. "I think beating 'em at this point would be enough. It'd prove that we're ready to move up in this league. Other teams would have to start taking us more seriously."

"*Are* we ready?" Zach asked.

"I don't know," Rachel said. "But we'll find out tomorrow."

After everyone had gone home and Andy had helped his mother pack the car, she handed him a small box.

"What is it?" he asked.

"Happy birthday," she said.

Andy's puzzlement turned to delight as he ripped off the wrapping paper and took a gold ring out of the box.

"The Championship ring!" he cried. "You really did it, Mom!"

"Well, Andy," she said. "I always promised that someday—when you were old enough—you would get your grandfather's Championship ring. Today, I think you're old enough. Happy birthday."

"You're the best, Mom," Andy said.

He held the massive baseball ring up high and watched it gleam. A large, red center stone was embedded in gold. Along the side the date 1954 stood out boldly. Inside the ring was the inscription "Swing from the heart."

Ike Rudolph, Andy's grandfather, had received the ring for playing on the team that won the 1954 semipro league Championship Series in their area. Andy had never really known him. Ike died when Andy was a baby. All Andy really knew was that Ike was a catcher—just like Andy—and that he had a quiet, strong manner.

"I like to think that you take after him," Mrs. West often told Andy.

In the car, on the way home, Andy was silent for a long time. Finally, he asked his mother:

"Did you ever see him play, Mom?"

"Only a couple of times," said Mrs. West. "I was little. He only played two more years after winning that Championship. That was his big moment. Then he injured his knees."

Andy looked down at his own knees. Then he gripped an imaginary bat with his hands.

"I'll bet he really socked 'em out of the park," Andy said. "Right, Mom?"

Mrs. West smiled. "He was a wonderful man," she said. "He was a wonderful father."

2 A Cloud of Dust

A crowd surrounded Andy West on Saturday morning before the game at Bloom Field. As he took the Championship ring out of its box there was a hush.

"Holy samolee!" Zach Langlin cried. "You got it!"

"Outrageous!" Rachel said.

"Rowff!" barked H.P., wagging his tail briskly.

"Is that thing for real?" shortstop Ernie Peters asked.

" 'Course it's for real," Zach said. "Didn't you know Andy's grandpa was on a team that won the semipro Championship Series?"

"They give you a gold ring for winning the Championship Series?" first baseman Marty Franklin asked.

"What else would they give you," Zach said, brushing back his blond hair with his cap, "a popcorn necklace?"

"It must be worth a fortune!" Seth Bradigan said.

Andy moved in closer. "As a matter of fact," he said in a low voice, "see that man over there sitting in back of my mom?"

Everyone turned and saw a man in the stands wearing sunglasses and a red fishing hat.

"He's a baseball *what's-it* collector," Andy said.

"Memorabilia?" Rachel suggested. She loved big fancy words.

"Yeah, that's it," Andy said. "A baseball memorabilia collector. Mr. Hudson's in town for the big baseball memorabilia show next week. He buys and sells old baseball stuff."

"Like what?" asked Seth.

"Like Babe Ruth's bat. And Reggie Jackson's socks," answered Andy. "In fact, he just offered my mom some money for this ring. It seems he has a special collection of semipro Championship rings and pennants from the nineteen-fifties."

"No fooling," Seth said. "What'd your mother tell him?"

Andy smiled. "She told him to ask me. It's my ring. And *I* told him to buzz off, but in a nice way. I wouldn't sell this ring for a zillion bucks!"

"Good for you," a voice said. It was Big Joe Jones. He was third baseman for the Mudsharks.

"What are *you* doing here?" Rachel asked him.

"Just came over to check out the merchandise," Big Joe said, taking the ring in his hand. "Where'd a guy like you ever get a hold of a thing like this, West?"

"It was my grandpa's," Andy said.

"Your grandpa, eh," Big Joe said, squinting. "What'd he ever do?"

Rachel said, "Andy's grandfather Ike Rudolph was a catcher for the Lotus Pines Hawks that won the nineteen fifty-four Championship Series."

"Never heard of him," Joe said. "Probably 'cause he was a whiff artist like Andy here—always striking out or hitting cheesy little pop-ups."

Andy's normally calm eyes suddenly flared. "As a matter of fact," he said, "my grandpa was a *tremendous* hitter. His homer in the ninth inning won the fourth game of the nineteen fifty-four Series."

"All the more reason a real power hitter like me should own it," Big Joe said. "This ring should belong to a hitter. Not to a misser. What d'you say, West? I'll give you ten bucks for the thing. Plus my Bo Jackson bat. Plus my All-Star Baseball video cartridge. Hey, I'll even give you free hitting lessons if you want."

"Take a hike!" Rachel said, pushing him away.

H.P. backed Rachel up with a couple of brave barks.

"I'm serious here," Big Joe said. "What would it take for you to give it up? Honest, West."

Now Seth Bradigan stepped in.

"Give the ring back," Seth said. He was fairly tall, with a solid, athletic build.

11

"Oh yeah," Big Joe said. "What if I don't?"

With Seth on his tiptoes, the two stood chest to chest, neither one of them giving ground. Then the umpire suddenly stepped in.

"What's going on here?" the ump asked. He was a huge man. With his mask, chest protector, and pockets full of baseballs he towered over the players like a big bear.

"This guy won't give Andy back his ring," Rachel said, pointing to Joe Jones.

"Is that true?" the umpire asked Andy.

"Everything's okay," Andy said.

"Wow, that's some ring," the umpire said, taking the ring from Big Joe. "Where did you get it, son?"

"Andy's grandfather was Ike Rudolph," Zach said.

The umpire's face lit up. "Ike Rudolph—the catcher?" he said. Andy nodded. "No fooling. I remember him. He played for the Hawks in the nineteen-fifties. Clutch hitter. He had an arm like a cannon."

By now everyone had scattered except for Andy. The umpire took one last look at the ring, then handed it back to him. "You take good care of this thing, you hear?" the umpire said with a smile.

"I will," Andy said, as he walked back to the bench.

The Slugger's batting order went like this:

Player	Position	Bats/Throws	Batting Avg.
Rachel Langlin	Right Field	Right/Right	.316
Susan Stein	Center Field	Right/Right	.296
Seth Bradigan	Left Field	Right/Right	.385
Marty Franklin	First Base	Left/Left	.275
Michelle Brooks	Third Base	Right/Right	.265
Luis Diaz	Second Base	Right/Right	.262
Andy West	Catcher	Right/Right	.146
Ernie Peters	Shortstop	Right/Both	.261
Zach Langlin	Pitcher	Left/Left	.245

It was rapidly becoming a solid lineup. The only player who wasn't hitting consistently was Andy. The hard-swinging catcher had been in a slump all season.

When Rachel ripped a double to lead off the game, and Susan followed with a single, it looked like the Sluggers were going to get a jump on the Mudsharks.

But then Seth Bradigan, normally the team's most dependable hitter, just got under the ball and hit a towering pop-up for the first out. Marty Franklin followed with a fly-out deep to right.

Michelle Brooks was then lucky enough to draw a walk and load the bases. Luis was even luckier to be struck lightly on the foot with a pitch to drive in a run.

"An RBI! All *right*!" Luis cried, as he limped down to first base. His foot stung a little, but it was okay. That left things up to Andy. A hit here could really break the game wide open.

As Andy stepped into the box he had several things on his mind. First was his season-long slump. He hadn't really got hold of a pitch once this year.

"Hey, no batter up there!" Big Joe called to his teammates. "It's West. Everyone move way in!"

Andy gritted his teeth. Was he going to let a guy like Big Joe spoil his concentration?

The answer, of course, was to do what the coach always told him—cut down on his swing. Make contact.

But then he looked down at the Championship Series ring on his left hand. It was too big for him, yet Andy hadn't been able to wait to wear it. It sparkled in the warm sunlight.

Then the question occurred to him:

Was Ike Rudolph the type of guy who would settle for just making contact? Was that how he hit the monster homer to win the game in the Championship Series—by cutting down on his swing?

"No way!" Andy mumbled to himself. When the pitch came in he swung wildly from his heels—and belted it!

The ball flew over the center fielder's head on a line and bashed into the fence. Susan, Michelle, and Luis all scored. With a little more speed, Andy might have had a grand slam. As it was, he was plenty happy with a bases-clearing triple.

"Way to go!" several of Andy's teammates called from the bench.

H.P. celebrated by running up and down the sideline — barking and wagging his tail.

"You can open your eyes now, West!" he heard Big Joe say. "That was the luckiest stroke I ever saw!"

Andy looked down at his ring and smiled.

With a 4–0 lead, the Sluggers took the field in the bottom of the first. For the first pitch, Andy stuck one finger down for a fastball. Zach reared back and fired.

"Stee-rike one!" the umpire bellowed.

"Yow!" Andy cried.

"Something wrong, son?" the umpire asked through his mask. Andy shook his head. His ring finger stung like a hot potato!

For the next pitch he called for a change-up. That didn't hurt so much. But the pattern was clear. Every time Zach threw his fastball, Andy's finger went numb with pain.

With two out and a runner on second, Big Joe came up. Andy signaled for a change-up.

"Time!" Zach called. He was popping bubble gum bubbles furiously. That usually meant he was upset. Andy went out to the mound for a conference.

"What are you trying to do to me?" Zach asked him. "My fastball's really hopping today. Why aren't you calling for it?"

"Big Joe really swings for the fences," Andy said. "I thought we could fool him with some slow stuff."

Andy went back behind the plate and called for a

change-up. Big Joe wasn't fooled at all. He hit a screamer down the left-field line for a two-run homer.

Andy had learned his lesson. For the next batter he called for three fastballs, and Zach struck him out.

After the Sluggers failed to score in the second, Andy tried a different strategy when he took the field. This time he put the ring on his throwing hand so the fastballs wouldn't hurt.

The strategy worked fine until the fourth inning. Then, with a score of 4–3 and runners on first and second, the Mudsharks dropped a bunt right in front of the plate.

Andy picked up the ball, flung off his mask, and rose to make the throw to third to catch the lead runner.

Without the ring, it would have been a fairly easy play. With the ring, he couldn't grip the ball correctly. The throw went sailing into left field, allowing the lead runner to score.

Coach Terwilliger scratched his head. Normally Andy's defense was good and his hitting was bad. Today, the opposite seemed to be true.

The Mudsharks scored another run with a sharp single to left by catcher Chip Hoover. That put them up 5–4. By the sixth inning the score was still the same. But now Andy had moved the ring to his back pants pocket for safekeeping.

Just before coming to bat in the top of the last inning, Andy took out his ring and rubbed it for luck.

He hadn't got hold of a pitch since the first inning. His second time up he took three huge cuts and struck out. In the fourth, he took another big swing and hit a feeble pop-up.

Now, with two outs and Luis Diaz on third base, Andy had the game riding on his bat. Andy took two big swings for two big strikes. Seeing a third mighty swing make contact, the Mudsharks' left fielder just naturally backed up. By the time he realized that Andy had just topped the ball weakly, the ball fell in over third for a lucky single.

Andy's hit had tied the score!

On first base, Andy took out his ring again. This was the way Ike Rudolph did it, he imagined. He wanted to believe that they both used big, powerful swings to come through in clutch situations.

With the score tied at 5–5 in the bottom of the sixth, the Southside Sluggers had to hold on. But things didn't look too good. Big Joe was coming to the plate.

"Been thinking about my offer for that ring, West?" Joe asked Andy.

Andy felt for the ring. It was tucked deep inside his back pocket. Andy pulled it out and put it on his right hand.

"No thanks," Andy said, patting his ring with pride.

"Let's cut the chatter, boys," the umpire said, as the pitch came spinning in.

Big Joe swung and lashed a sharp double to right.

Now Zach had to bear down. Any more hits here and the game would be over. On a three-ball, two-strike count, Zach struck out the Mudsharks' left fielder Phil Woods with a wicked fast ball.

"Way to go!" Andy cried. "Two more, Zach! Two more!"

The Mudsharks' Joan Jeffers swung at the first pitch and flied out to Susan Stein in deep center field. Then, it looked like the Sluggers had a good chance to get out of the inning when Mike Moran popped weakly to shallow left.

"Clear out!" yelled a speeding Seth Bradigan, as he motioned shortstop Ernie Peters away from the blooper. But the ball was hit too shallow, and Seth had to play it on one hop.

Seth saw Big Joe steamrolling around third. He cocked his right arm, and fired a low bullet toward home.

As the umpire crouched down to get a good view of the play, Andy flung his mask off with his right hand. Then he quickly braced himself for the collision with Big Joe.

The ball came speeding in, just as Big Joe launched into his slide. It thumped into Andy's mitt at the exact instant that Big Joe slammed into him.

Crash!!

The dust flew all over. And the umpire sprang to his feet so fast that a spare baseball came tumbling out of his open pocket.

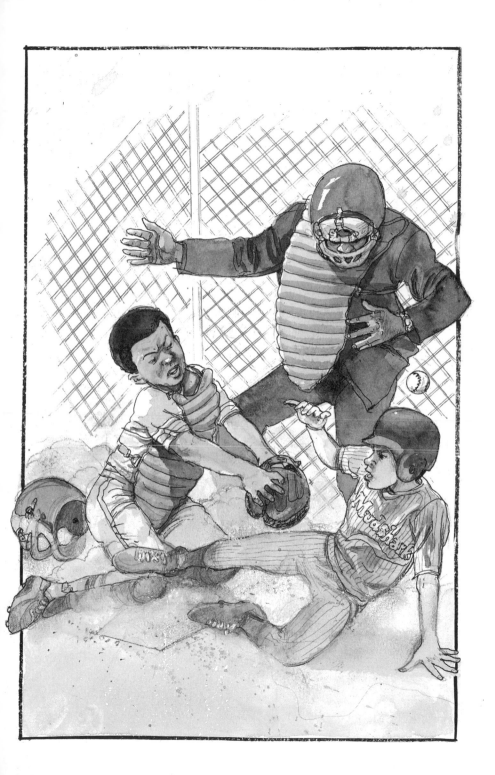

At first it looked like the ump was going to give the "out" sign with his right hand. But then his left arm shot out as well, and crossed over his right.

"*Safe!*" barked the ump.

"He dropped the ball!" Big Joe laughed.

Andy rolled over and held up the ball in his mitt.

Now Zach came running in, protesting the call.

"He didn't drop the ball!" he cried, holding up Andy's mitt. "See! Here it is!"

"Yes, he did!" shouted Chip Hoover, the first Mudshark to run out from the bench. "Andy picked the ball up out of the dirt."

Chip then scratched at the dirt around home plate for emphasis. He even held a fistful of dirt up to show the umpire.

"I've heard both sides now," the umpire barked. "He's still safe! He beat the throw. Another ball did fall on the ground, but it came from my pocket."

"But —" Zach griped.

"No *buts*, son," the umpire said. "The player was safe. The ball game's over."

In the middle of the confusion, Mr. Hudson, the baseball memorabilia collector, tapped Andy on the shoulder.

"Nice game," Mr. Hudson said, giving Andy's hand a firm squeeze. "That was one heck of a play you just made. Too bad it didn't work out."

"I'll say," Andy sighed, wanting to get back to arguing his case with the umpire.

"All you can do is keep trying," Mr. Hudson continued. "It's like me and that Championship ring. I didn't get it today, but I'll keep trying. I have a special place in my collection for semi-pro rings from the nineteen-fifties. They remind me of the teams I watched when I was about your age. You let me know if you change your mind, Son."

"Right," Andy said, as he watched Mr. Hudson walk away into the crowd.

Andy then turned around to speak to the ump again. He knew he couldn't win the argument now, but he was too upset to just give up. Seth, Zach, and Rachel were also talking to the umpire. After a minute or so, the umpire finally just shrugged and walked away with his equipment.

Somehow, it seemed, Grandpa Ike's ring had let Andy down at the last moment. Andy sighed and casually reached over to twist the ring on his finger.

"It's gone!" he cried, studying his hand and the ground around him. "It's gone!!"

"What's gone?" Seth asked, stepping toward him.

Andy ran through the crowd looking for the man in the red fisherman's hat. He even ran out to the parking lot. But, finally, he gave up and trudged back to his friends.

"It was him," Andy sighed, trying to hold back the tears. "He did it!"

"Who?" Seth asked. "Who did what?"

"Mr. Hudson, the baseball memorabilia guy," Andy said. "He took my ring."

3 Suspects

"Mr. Hudson took your ring?" Rachel gasped. "Are you sure you didn't just forget where you put it?"

Andy wriggled off his chest protector and tossed his mask and catcher's mitt right on top of home plate. Then he turned all his pockets inside-out.

"Nothing," he said.

"Maybe you just lost it," Zach said.

"I don't think I lost it," Andy said glumly. "I think Mr. Hudson took it. After the game. When he shook my hand."

"Wait a second," Zach said. "Do you realize what you're saying here?"

"I know what I'm saying," Andy cried. "That man took my grandpa's Championship ring!"

"What about the collision?" Zach suggested. "Have you checked around here? Maybe the ring got knocked into the ground during the play at the plate."

Andy bent over and grabbed up his mask and mitt. Then he tossed the equipment off to the side and crouched down over home plate.

"I'll find that ring if it's here," Andy cried, as he dug up the dirt around home with his fingers.

"Stop, Andy!" Rachel insisted. "Let's do this scientifically."

"Like how?" Zach asked with a smile.

"Scientifically," Rachel repeated. "Everyone spread out. Zach, take next to the backstop. Andy, you look *calmly* around home plate. Seth and I will take the baselines."

Everyone knelt down and sifted through the dirt. They worked swiftly but carefully.

While everyone was pawing through the dust, Big Joe and Chip Hoover walked by. They were both licking green ice pops. H.P. growled at them and then trotted over to Zach.

"Hey, Joe," Chip said, "get a load of this. It's the Southside Sluggers, playin' in the dirt. Hey, don't you guys know there's a sandbox over in the playground?"

Joe and Chip roared with laughter.

"Seriously, though, West," Big Joe said with a smile, "what the heck are you birds doing down there? Hunting for the baseball? You couldn't get a hold of it to make the big play. So why bother looking for it now?"

"Give 'em a baseball, Joe," Chip said, laughing. "They can tag each other out."

"Very funny," Rachel snapped. "We're looking for Andy's Championship ring. Have either of you seen it?"

Joe searched through his pockets. "Hey, wait a second," he said, with a surprised smile. "What's this?"

There was a gasp as Joe pulled something small and shiny out of his pocket.

"Aw," he said, pretending to be sorry. "Too bad. It's only a shiny penny. And here I thought it was a Championship ring. Well, better luck next time, West."

"Yeah, sure," Andy said.

A moment after the two Mudsharks left, Seth announced that he was quitting the search.

"It's not here, Andy," he said. "We've looked everywhere. The ring just isn't here. Can you think of anyplace else you might have left it?"

Andy stood up and shook his head. His eyes welled with tears. He was about to say something. Then he just grabbed his equipment bag and ran off.

Rachel, Zach, Seth, and H.P. caught up with Andy at the big oak tree, the place they always used when they had to think things out. Andy was staring at the ground, pulling up weeds with a blank expression on his face.

"Andy," Rachel said quietly.

Andy didn't answer. He just kept pulling up weeds.

"Andy, you've got to let us help you," Seth said.

Andy's face brightened for a second. Then he looked down again and continued pulling weeds.

"Seth's right," Zach said. "That ring's not lost. We'll find it. We'll get it back."

"How?" Andy asked.

Zach looked over at Rachel. "Well, come on," he said. "Think of a plan."

"I'm thinking," Rachel said.

"Wait a second," Zach said. "I've got it. We'll call the police. They'll put out a what-do-you-call-it. An all-points bulletin."

"We can't call the police," Andy said.

"Why not?" Zach said.

"Because Andy's not sure whether the ring was lost or stolen," Rachel said.

"Oh," Zach said.

"Well how 'bout this," Seth said. "We call up Mr. What's-his-name. Mr. Hudson. And we say, 'Hand over that ring, buster. We know you took it.'"

"And what if he says he doesn't have it?" Rachel said. "Then what do we do?"

"H-m-m," Seth said, scratching his chin. "I see what you mean. It's our word against his. So what do we do, Sherlock?"

"Well," Rachel said, "the first thing we've got to do is go over what happened. Then take it from there."

"There's nothing to go over," Andy said. "I had the

ring. Then I talked to Mr. Hudson. Then it was gone."

"Well, hold on," Seth said. "Did you *see* him take the ring?"

Andy shook his head.

"Well," Seth continued. "Did you *feel* him take it?"

Andy threw up his hands.

"I'm not sure of anything anymore," he said. "I'm not sure if I even *had* the ring when I was speaking to Mr. Hudson."

"All right," Rachel said. "Let's go over exactly what happened on that play at home plate—real slowly! Let's see. Big Joe was on second, right?"

"Right," Andy said. "And Mike Moran was up."

"What'd you do when he hit the ball?" Rachel asked.

"What I always do," Andy said. "I stood up. And I kicked the bat out of the way so no one would trip over it."

"Which hand was the ring on?" Seth asked.

Andy thought for a moment.

"My left," he said. "No—my right. I put the ring on my throwing hand when Big Joe came up to bat."

"Then what?" Seth asked.

"Well, you know," Andy said. "Mike hit the ball out to you, Seth—"

Seth stood and scooped up an invisible baseball on one short hop.

"And I made the perfect pickup," Seth said.

"Meanwhile, Big Joe was rounding third," Andy said.

"And I wound up and fired a bullet home," Seth said, heaving the invisible ball with all his might.

"And I whipped off my catcher's mask and got ready to make the tag at the plate," Andy said. "The ball zipped into my glove just as Big Joe crashed into me."

"Good thing my throw was right on target," Seth cried. "What a throw!"

"Then Big Joe said Andy dropped the ball," Rachel added. "And the umpire had already called Joe safe."

"Yeah, then I came running in to argue the call," Zach said. "And showed the umpire that the ball was still in the pocket of Andy's mitt."

Zach ran over and held up the invisible ball.

"Then we all got untangled," Andy said. "And that was about it."

"Whew," Zach said. "Makes me tired, just talkin' about that play."

"Was anybody else there?" Rachel asked, while playing with a pencil.

"Why do you want to know?" Andy said.

"I'm trying to make a list of suspects," she said, opening her notebook. "So far we have Mr. Hudson, Big Joe, and who else?"

She looked at Zach.

"I can think of two other suspects," Zach said. "How about the umpire? He was right there."

"And he really seemed to love that ring," Seth added.

"Nah, umpires like Mr. Joyner wouldn't steal,"

Andy said, rejecting the idea completely. "Mr. Joyner's a good guy. Who's your other suspect?"

"Me," Zach said.

"You!" everyone cried.

"Well," Zach said sheepishly. "I know it sounds wild. But I was really the only other person to run in there. And maybe, when we got all tangled up, I accidentally swallowed it or it got stuck in my hat or something."

Rachel slammed her notebook. H.P. looked up in surprise and then settled back down again.

"Who votes that what Zach just said is the most ridiculous thing they ever heard in their life?" she said.

All four hands shot up—including Zach's.

"Then it's unanimous," Rachel said. "Can we get back to solving this?"

"Solving what?" Andy said. "I don't think there are any more suspects. I think Mr. Hudson took the ring."

"Or maybe Big Joe," Seth said.

"Or maybe Chip Hoover," Zach added. "He was the first Mudshark to run over after the play. Chip could have found the ring on the ground. Remember how he scratched at the dirt around home plate. And held up a fistful of dirt for the umpire."

"Chip can be mean at times—like Big Joe," Andy said. "But my top suspect is still Mr. Hudson."

"I agree," Rachel said. "We should check out Mr. Hudson first. But how do we do it?"

* * *

Almost an hour later Zach returned from the refreshment stand with four big foamy root beers.

"Well, have you gotten any farther on the plan?" he asked, as he passed out the root beers.

Rachel turned back a few pages in her notebook and began to read.

"Question number one," she began. "Could we possibly think it was an honest mistake? That Mr. Hudson took the ring by accident?"

"Maybe," Seth said. "It could've been an accident."

"Nah," Andy jumped in. "You can't accidentally slip a ring off somebody's hand and then walk away without being aware of it."

"True," Rachel said, licking the foam off her root beer. "If Mr. Hudson has the ring, it was no accident."

"So, just asking him for the ring is out?" asked Zach.

"Obviously," Rachel said with a smirk. "He's not just going to admit he's a crook and hand the ring over."

"Then how can we find out if he took it?" Zach asked.

"We have to set a trap," Rachel said, closing her notebook.

"What kind of a trap?" Andy asked.

"A Championship ring trap," Rachel said with a sly smile. "What else?"

"How do you make a Championship ring trap?" Seth asked.

"Well, Rachel said, "the first thing we'll need is a newspaper."

"A newspaper!" Andy cried. "You're going to get my ring back with a newspaper! How is that possible?"

"Don't worry," Rachel said. "You'll see."

4 Fishing for Clues

Everyone on the team knew that Coach Terwilliger loved fishing. But it still seemed peculiar when he came to the practice field on Wednesday carrying a fishing rod.

"Good idea," Zach said. "It's too hot to practice today anyway."

"Yeah," Seth said. "Let's go fishing. Where do you want to go, Coach? How about Crystal Lake?"

"How about right here?" the coach said.

"Right here?" Zach said. "You mean the pond?"

"No," the coach said. "I mean right here." He pointed to the practice field with his rod and reel.

"I don't get it," Seth said.

"Me either," said Marty Franklin. "There's no hook on that line."

"We don't need a hook. We're going to talk about hitting today," the coach said.

"With a *fishing* pole?" Luis laughed.

The coach nodded. "What I need now," he said, "is a fish. Anyone got a fish, by any chance?"

Susan Stein reached in her bag and pulled out a small stuffed animal.

"I've got a crocodile," she said.

"Perfect," the coach said. "We'll go crocodile fishing."

He took the stuffed crocodile and laid it on the grass. It was about one hundred feet away along the third-base line.

H.P., the Sluggers' mascot, sniffed around the toy crocodile and then hunkered down by the bench to watch the action.

"Now," the coach said. "I'll need a volunteer to catch the crocodile. Zach. You ever used a rod and reel before?"

Zach shook his head. "Not really," he said.

"Good," the coach said, handing Zach the fishing rod. "Now this is what I want you to do, Zach. Cast the line. See if you can catch the crocodile."

"But it's too far away," Zach said.

"Go ahead," the coach encouraged. "Really swing it out there. Stand back, everyone."

Zach took a mighty heave but the metal sinker on the end of the line hardly went anywhere. He tried again and again. The harder he swung, the shorter the distance his casts traveled.

"That's enough, Zach," the coach said.

Zach stood up and took a bow.

"Thank you, thank you," he said, grinning.

"Now I need another volunteer," the coach said. "Susan—you know anything about crocodile fishing?"

Susan laughed. The coach gave her the rod and told her to cast. Only this time he gave her some advice.

"Swing easy," he said. "Let the weight of the sinker carry the line out there."

Susan's first few casts didn't go very far. But then, after a while, she got the hang of it. She began to smoothly flick the rod with a gentle motion. The sinker drifted out farther and farther until it finally hit the crocodile.

"Bingo!" the coach said. "Nice shot, Susan."

He took the rod from her and set it down.

"Now you see the importance of a smooth, easy swing," the coach said. "Susan cast only half as hard as Zach—but the line went twice as far.

"Yeah," Seth shouted. "But we're playing baseball. We're not trout fishing!"

"It's the same when you hit a baseball," Coach Terwilliger replied. "If you swing too hard—what happens?"

"You don't catch any crocodiles," Zach answered.

Everyone laughed.

"Andy?" the coach said, pointing to the catcher who had raised his hand.

"You strike out," Andy said in a low voice. "Just the way I do when I overswing."

"Right," the coach said. "You've got it, Andy. Now, ten swings each, everyone. And remember, if you want to catch a crocodile, swing easy."

The Sluggers all ran out to their positions. Only Andy stayed behind. He picked up the fishing rod and hefted it. Then, after he was sure no one was watching, he tried a mighty cast.

Poof!

The sinker landed only about ten feet in front of him, right at Seth's feet.

"C'mon, Andy," Seth said. "I want to bat. We're waiting for you to get your catcher's gear on."

"Oh, right," Andy said. "I'll be right over."

Crouched behind the plate Andy thought about hitting. Did the good hitters really cut down on their swings to make contact?

He watched his friend Seth step into the batter's box. Robin Hayes, the Sluggers' relief pitcher, was just lobbing the ball over the plate. Somehow, when Seth swung hard, it looked easy.

Or was it the other way around? Seth's swing was so easy that it looked hard.

As Andy kept watching, he thought he began to notice a pattern. Sometimes, it seemed, Seth really laid into Robin's pitches. And other times, all he seemed to be going for was a solid connection.

"Hey, Seth," Andy said through his catcher's mask.

"Do you swing hard at every pitch?"

"Sometimes I swing hard," Seth said, sending a drive to the alley in left center.

"What about the other times?" Andy asked.

Seth took another pitch and poled it over the fence in center for a home run.

"Like I said," Seth said. "Sometimes I swing hard. And other times—I swing smooth as glass."

When Andy's turn came to bat, he missed the first five pitches. The more he missed, the harder he swung. The harder he swung, the more he missed.

On the fifth pitch, he swung so hard he popped a belt loop.

"This is getting ridiculous," he told Zach, who was waiting his turn to bat behind the backstop. "If only I had my ring. I was really hitting some shots when I had that ring."

"I think you're the one that's getting ridiculous," Zach said. "If you think a ring can help you hit."

"Why not?" Andy said.

When the next pitch came in he was so busy talking about the ring that he forgot to tense up. As a result, he socked a liner that whistled right down the third-base line, knocking what looked like a big clump of sod into the air.

"Hey, that's Susan's crocodile," Zach said. "Nice shot, Andy! I hope you didn't hurt the poor thing."

Andy smiled. "See what I mean?" he asked. "Just *talking* about that ring improves my hitting."

* * *

After practice Andy, Rachel, Seth, and Zach agreed to meet at the Southside Ice Cream Shop. Each was to bring exactly one dollar and eighty-seven cents. In addition, Rachel had to stop to buy a newspaper.

Andy, Rachel, and Zach were already waiting when Seth came in and plopped his $1.87 on the table.

Andy added it to the rest of the money.

"Good," he said, adding an extra two cents. "That makes exactly seven dollars and fifty cents. Now what are we going to do with it?"

"It's the registration fee for the Lotus Pines Baseball Memorabilia Show," said Rachel.

She held out the registration form she'd cut out of the newspaper.

"But why register in the Lotus Pines Baseball Memorabilia Show?" Andy asked.

"Because Mr. Hudson's going to be there," Rachel replied. "You told us that yourself when you first pointed him out at the game. 'Mr. Hudson's in town for the big baseball memorabilia show,' you said."

"I know that," Andy said. "What I want to know is why are *we* going to register in the show?"

"We're not," Seth said.

Andy threw up his hands. "Well, then—who is?"

"David Kramer," Rachel said.

"Now you've lost me too," Zach said. "Who's David Kramer?"

"He's a baseball collector," Seth said. "Mostly he's got baseball cards."

"All of us have baseball cards too!" Zach said.

"Oh, I get it. There is no David Kramer. Is there?"

"We made him up," Rachel said. "He's part of the trap."

"It's sort of like going fishing," Seth said. "The idea is to lure Mr. Hudson into revealing whether he's got the ring or not."

"What's the bait?" Andy asked.

"A bunch of fairly rare baseball cards," Seth said.

"*What* rare cards?" Zach cried. "We don't have a bunch of cards to trade away." Then he thought about it for a second.

"Oh, I see," Zach said. "There is no bunch of rare cards, is there? We're just pretending."

"You got it," Seth said.

"So what do we do?" Andy wondered. "An invisible David Kramer walks up to Mr. Hudson and says, 'Hey, you want to trade for these invisible cards?'"

"Sort of," Rachel chuckled. "We put up a notice on the bulletin board. It says we're interested in trading for a nineteen-fifties semipro Championship ring. If Mr. Hudson comes with your ring—we've *got* him!"

"The beauty of the plan," Seth said, "is that you can catch more than one fish with the same bait."

"How's that?" Andy asked.

"Suppose Mr. Hudson *doesn't* have the ring," Seth said. "But someone else does."

"Oh, I get it," Andy said. "Whoever's got the ring will go for the bait. And then we'll have 'em."

"Exactly," Seth said. "Even somebody like Big Joe collects cards and might be at the show."

"I don't know," Andy said. "Isn't it wrong to pretend that we're someone we're not?"

"How else are you going to get your ring back?" Seth said.

Rachel shook her head.

"Of course, it would be better if we didn't have to pretend to be David Kramer," Rachel added. "But if we use our own names, whoever took the ring would recognize us."

"What happens when Mr. Hudson wants to *meet* Mr. Kramer," Zach said. "Then what do we do?"

"That's a good question," Rachel said. "One of us could pretend to be David Kramer, but if he suspects something's wrong, the deal's over. So it's tricky. If anybody has any ideas . . ."

"I've got an idea," Zach said. "It's kind of wild, but . . ."

"Well?" Rachel said, impatiently.

The three other Sluggers gathered around Zach.

"We're all ears," Seth said.

5 Operation Fudgebar

The name of Zach's plan was "Operation Fudgebar."

"Operation Fudgebar?" Everyone groaned.

"That's right, Operation Fudgebar," Zach said. "With the accent on the *fudge*."

The first thing needed for Operation Fudgebar was some photographic equipment—a camera, film, things like that. This was no problem, as photography had been one of Zach's favorite hobbies since the third grade.

The second thing Zach needed was Rachel's baseball card catalogue.

"What exactly are you going to do with the catalogue?" Rachel asked.

"I'm just going to take photos of the cards," Zach

said. "Of course, I'll have to cut the cards out of the catalogue first."

Inside the catalogue were pictures of valuable baseball cards—dozens of them. Full-size and in full color. They were the perfect kind of pictures to make fake baseball cards out of. And that's what Operation Fudgebar was—a plan to make fake baseball cards.

The pictures in Rachel's catalogue would be cut out, photographed and then mounted on a large poster. This would be David Kramer's poster for the memorabilia show. It would show off his "somewhat valuable baseball card collection." It would also be the perfect bait for catching a Championship ring thief.

"Operation Fudgebar," Zach said, "is how we're going to get the ring back from Mr. Hudson."

"How?" Rachel said.

"The poster will say that David Kramer wants to trade his cards for a nineteen-fifties semipro Championship ring," Zach said.

"Here," Rachel grumped, handing Zach her catalogue. "I think I'm going to regret I ever heard of Operation Fudgebar in the first place."

"It's the only way," Zach said.

"Why is it the only way?" Rachel asked.

"You said so yourself," Zach said. "Because if we go there ourselves, he'll recognize us."

"What if we wear disguises?" Rachel asked.

"Get real," Andy said. "What kind of disguises could we use—cowboy and cowgirl suits? You think he wouldn't figure out who it was in two seconds?"

Seth laughed.

"And anyway," Zach said. "Operation Fudgebar makes David Kramer seem more real."

"Let's think this through one more time," Rachel said. "Suppose Operation Fudgebar works perfectly. How do we know Mr. Hudson's got Andy's ring?"

"The poster will have instructions," Zach said. "It'll say: 'Describe the ring completely, including inscriptions. Place description in message box.'"

"What if Mr. Hudson won't trade?" Rachel asked.

"He'll trade," Zach said. "He's a memorabilia collector. That's what they do."

"Zach's right," Andy said. "I'm sure he'll trade for that ring."

"So all we have to do," Zach said, "is offer cards that are valuable enough to tempt him. Cards that add up to a fair swap for that ring."

"Hey, look at this," Seth said, holding up Rachel's catalogue. "Howard Johnson's rookie card. This thing will get his attention."

"Perfect!" Zach cried.

"Yeah," Rachel said. "Except that's not really a baseball card. It's just a *picture* of a baseball card."

"That's why we have to do this just right," Zach said. "To make Operation Fudgebar look completely real."

By Friday afternoon, Operation Fudgebar was under way. Sixteen different cards were cut out—

including Howard Johnson's and Darryl Strawberry's rookie cards. To make them look thick, each one had been pasted to the front of a real but far less valuable baseball card. Then Zach set up the lighting and the backdrop for the photographs.

"Say 'cheese,'" Zach joked, as he clicked off several exposures. "If we're lucky, the enlargements should be ready by tomorrow. They should make one great poster."

After dinner that night, Andy was quiet. He was worried about Sunday's game against the Bluesox. Andy hoped his slump was over. The ring certainly had seemed to help him get two big hits against the Mudsharks.

Andy also worried about Operation Fudgebar. Could a wild plan like that really work?

"Andy?" called his mother from the front porch.

Andy's mother liked to sit out during warm evenings and listen to the crickets. Andy went out and sat next to her on the steps.

"You seem so serious tonight," Mrs. West said with concern in her voice. "Like your grandfather used to be."

Andy shrugged. The mere mention of his grandfather brought a twinge of guilt.

"Tell me what you remember about the way Grandpa played," Andy said. "Was he a real power hitter?"

Mrs. West shook her head.

"It's all so foggy now," she said. "There is one thing I remember, though. In a local magazine article I read. They called him 'The Rock.'"

"'The Rock'?" Andy echoed.

"That sounds funny, I know," Mrs. West said with a smile. "But it made sense. That's the way he was. Solid as a rock. My mom always said how dependable he was."

"Do you have any idea where that article was?" Andy asked.

"Why no," Mrs. West said. "Why do you ask?"

"Oh, nothing," Andy said. "I've just been thinking. Maybe I should learn more about Grandpa."

"Why don't you go to the library tomorrow?" Mrs. West said. "They have lots of old local newspapers and magazines."

"That's a good idea," Andy said. Then he looked at his watch. "I think I'll turn in early tonight."

"Okay Andy," Mrs. West said, giving him a hug.

As Andy drifted off to sleep he imagined Ike Rudolph looming over his bed.

"Swing from the heart," Ike seemed to be telling him.

Andy smiled. That's what he'd do. On Sunday he'd really swing from the heart—and hit a few out. That would make him feel a whole lot better.

The Bluesox had beaten the Sluggers badly the last time

they played. It was almost as if the Sluggers had been their old bumbling selves from last year—the team that had only won two games all season.

But this year the Sluggers were playing a lot better ball. They had beaten the Burger House Bulls and the Lampland Lasers. They had also played top teams like the Toyshop Tigers and the Rocket Raiders a bit closer this year.

"Let's look sharp!" Coach Terwilliger shouted to his team as they trotted onto the field. "Concentrate out there!"

In the top of the first, Zach walked the leadoff batter. This was followed by a groundout, a single, and a fly-out.

The sixth batter just got a chip out of Zach's fastball and popped it up behind the plate. Andy leaped to his feet. With his right hand, he tore off his mask and searched the sky for the ball. When he located it, he threw the mask in the opposite direction. This made sure that if he misjudged the ball he wouldn't trip over his own mask.

As the mask left his hand, Andy felt a twinge of something on his ring finger. It didn't really hurt. It was more like a ghost-pain—the memory of a pain you once had and expect to have again.

The ring, Andy suddenly thought, as he positioned himself for the catch. *It's like it's still on my hand. Still bringing me Grandpa's luck.*

The ball fell into Andy's outstretched mitt.

"Nice grab," Zach said to him, as the two ran in to the bench. "Let's get some hits now. Okay?"

Andy nodded. He couldn't wait to get a chance. He really felt his grandpa was still with him.

Albie Freedman was pitching for the Bluesox. Albie had good control, and he was smart and tricky. What he didn't have was a very strong fastball.

"Perfect," Andy muttered to himself, as he watched Albie retire the first three Slugger batters with a good mix of well-placed pitches and slow stuff. "Just the kind of pitcher I can really tee off on."

In the second inning the Bluesox scored twice. They had a couple of solid hits over third and first. In both cases the Sluggers made things worse with an error. Even sure-handed Rachel let a ball roll through her legs in right field.

"That's okay, Rach!" Andy shouted with a surprising degree of confidence. "We'll definitely get 'em back next inning!"

But the second inning for the Sluggers was pretty much the same as the first. Three Slugger batters came up, and three went down.

"Come on, everyone. Let's get cracking!" Andy shouted. "Give me something to work with."

Now he was going to have to wait one more inning just to get his first at bat. This was too much!

Even worse, the Bluesox jumped out to a 5–0 lead in the third when Tommy Asaki homered with two on base.

"It's up to me," Andy mumbled to himself, as he stepped up to the plate to lead off the third.

His warm-up swings were cool and menacing. Yet the hitting advice from his coach, from Seth, Rachel, and Zach swirled around in his brain.

"Make contact!" Andy heard the coach say.

"Just meet the ball," Rachel would chime in.

But a much louder and more tempting voice had the opposite message: "Swing from the heart, Andy."

Andy felt a warm rush of confidence wash over him. He glared out at the pitcher.

Come on, he challenged silently. *Show me what you've got!*

Albie's first pitch came floating in. It was like slow motion!

As Andy's bat lashed out there was a loud crack. The ball was definitely creamed! But it was foul by about twenty feet. So foul that no one got excited about it for even a second.

"Good rip, Andy!" Zach called from the bench.

Andy gritted his teeth. "Come on, try that again!" he jabbered under his breath to Albie.

Albie was only too glad to feed him another floater. This one was slower, trickier, and had more spin on it.

Whoosh! went Andy's bat.

"Stee-rike two!" called the umpire.

How did I miss *that thing?* Andy wondered, as he uncoiled himself.

Now he was mad. Albie Freedman was making him

look bad out here with his assortment of junk-balls. On this next pitch Andy was going to be smart. Instead of lurching at it he would wait. If the ball was slow, he would be even slower.

This would be a thing of perfection—*a swing from the heart*. Andy imagined Grandpa Ike smiling down at him now. Grandpa Ike would appreciate how Andy would finally get to this pitcher.

But Andy didn't get the slowball he expected. Instead, the ball came speeding in. Or, at least, it seemed to be speeding when compared with the last two pitches.

Andy's swing was smooth and powerful. Too bad it didn't really begin until after the ball had slammed into the catcher's mitt.

"Stee-rike three!" the umpire barked.

"Well, of all the . . ." Andy grumbled, as he walked back to the dugout. He just couldn't believe it.

Robin Hayes came into replace Zach on the mound in the top of the fourth inning. But the Sluggers didn't start to figure out Albie Freedman's pitching until the bottom of the fourth. After Rachel led off with a solid single to right, she shouted advice to her teammates.

"Just try to make contact!" Rachel yelled. "This guy's too tricky. You can't beat him by swinging for the fences."

Susan Stein followed Rachel's advice and came up with another hit. Now the Sluggers were rolling. And Albie was starting to act rattled. He walked Seth on four wild pitches. Then Marty doubled to right center, scoring two runs.

"We're coming back!" Zach shouted.

After Michelle flied out, Luis got to first on an error. This scored another run.

With runners on first and second, Andy came up again. This time he was determined not to get fooled.

Swing from the heart, he told himself, as he slashed at the first pitch.

"Stee-rike one!" the umpire barked.

After fouling another pitch off, Andy looked over at the coach. He clapped his hands three times, then touched each shoulder.

The signal for a hit-and-run play!

The idea was to have both base runners take off after the pitch. This forced the infielders to cover their bases, leaving huge holes for the batter to push a ground ball through.

This also forced the batter not to take a wild swing. All Andy needed to do was make contact—just tap a little ground ball.

"Let's go!" the coach shouted.

It should have been easy—and would have been— had Albie not served up such a fat pitch.

The ball looked a yard wide as it drifted home. Andy couldn't control himself. Just as the ball dropped, he wound up and took a gigantic windmill swing.

"Stee-rike three!" the umpire barked.

But the play wasn't over. The runners were still

going. Marty, who wasn't very fast, was only about halfway to third when the catcher's throw came zinging into the base. He was tagged out easily, ending what could have been a very big inning.

Andy threw down his bat. "Some swing from the heart!" he cried.

"What'd yuh say?" Ernie asked him.

"Oh, nothing," Andy said, fumbling with his gear.

Andy struck out one more time as the Sluggers lost the game, 7–4. Instead of swinging from the heart, he seemed to be swinging like a windmill.

6 Show Business

"May I help you?" the man behind the desk asked Rachel and Andy. His nameplate said M. SHERMAN. He was in charge of all the exhibits at the memorabilia show.

"Exhibit R-fifty-six," Andy said to Mr. Sherman.

Andy handed him the poster. It was now Tuesday and they'd spent hours Monday afternoon finishing it. Even Rachel had to admit, it looked pretty good. Under the picture was this message:

> I want to trade these cards for a 1954 SEMI-PRO CHAMPIONSHIP ring. Please leave a photo and/or description (including markings and inscriptions) of the ring in the message box. —DAVID KRAMER.

Mr. Sherman looked up R-56 in his little book.

"Ah, yes," he said to Andy. "Kramer, David. Fairly nice collection, Mr. Kramer," he said, looking at the cards on the poster. "You *are* Mr. Kramer, aren't you?"

"Uh—" Andy stuttered.

"That's okay," Mr. Sherman said. "You don't need to pretend anything here. Some of my best exhibitors are not much older than you two. That's the beauty of this business. You don't need to be old—or young—to be a collector. You just have to know memorabilia and love baseball."

Mr. Sherman was one of the biggest collectors in the county. His office was full of interesting items.

"Go ahead and look around if you like," Mr. Sherman told the two Sluggers. "I get a kick out of other collectors seeing my pieces."

The walls were covered with autographed photos of famous players. Shelves were filled with bats, balls, and parts of uniforms. Plastic-covered baseball cards were spread over Mr. Sherman's desk and several other tables. Rachel picked up an odd-looking costume that was draped over a chair.

"What's this?" she asked.

Mr. Sherman smiled. "A mascot costume," he chuckled. "The Minnesota Moose. I've got a Pittsburgh Snow Goose suit too. They're mascots for old minor-league teams."

"Are they valuable?" Rachel asked.

"Not really," Mr. Sherman said. "Why?"

"Oh, I was just wondering if we could borrow them for the show," Rachel said.

Andy jabbed her in the ribs. "Rachel!" he whispered.

"Whatever for?" Mr. Sherman asked.

"Well," Rachel said. "I was at this other baseball collector show. And they had mascots—just sort of walking around. For the kids, you know. And I was thinking. You wouldn't have to pay us or anything. Maybe just reduce the registration price a little—"

"Why, I think that's a wonderful idea," Mr. Sherman said.

"It is?" Andy said. "I mean—you do?"

"Of course," Mr. Sherman said. "In fact, I was actually thinking of hiring some more helpers myself."

Fifteen minutes later they were back outside, explaining the whole thing to Zach and Seth.

"You mean he's actually going to *pay* you to dress up like a goose and a moose?" Zach cried.

"That's right!" Andy said. "Mr. Sherman thought it was a good idea. The Moose and the Goose can roam around like ushers and help out with the show."

"But the big thing," Rachel said, "is that now we can go inside without being recognized. As long as we keep our masks on."

Zach pulled the goose mask over his head.

"*Honk honk! Honk! Hon-nnn-k!*" he cried. "Hey, this is terrific!"

With Operation Fudgebar now in place the four Sluggers went their separate ways. Zach went home to play video games. Seth was going to bike over to Plum Creek and look for crayfish. Rachel decided she would go to the pool and practice her backstroke.

"Want to come along?" she asked Andy.

"No, I'm going to the library," Andy said.

"The library?" she asked. "On a nice day like this?"

"Yeah," Andy said. "I've been meaning to look up some stuff."

At 5:00 P.M. sharp on Wednesday, the Moose and the Goose stood outside the auditorium with Zach and Seth.

"You look terrific," Zach said to the Goose. "How do you feel?"

"Hot," Rachel said.

"Me too," Andy moaned through his moose mask.

As they came through the door they were greeted by Mr. Sherman's announcement over the loudspeaker:

"*Welcome* to the Fifth Annual Lotus Pines Baseball Memorabilia Show!"

There were dozens of booths, tables, and bulletin boards. Banners and bunting were draped over the balcony. Balloons and confetti drifted from the ceiling. Paintings and photographs were posted everywhere. Crowds milled around, looking to buy or sell. Video displays hawked bats, balls, and autographs. Sporting-goods companies had set up live demonstrations.

The most crowded part of the room was Section R—the baseball card section. Rachel went straight there to see if poster R-56 was there.

It was! And she had to admit it looked great.

From there, she and the moose just wandered around. Their job was to pass out complimentary bubble gum and cards to kids under twelve.

Rachel took the left side of the room and Andy the right. Fortunately, R-56 was right near the middle, so they could both keep an eye on it.

After an hour of passing out bubble gum they met near the stage.

"Well?" Rachel said.

"Nothing," Andy said. "I just checked the message box at R-fifty-six. We've got several messages. But nobody yet mentioned a ring."

"You see anybody?" Rachel asked. Andy shook his head. "Me neither," Rachel said. "Oh, wait. There is one person—" She motioned to a boy in a baseball cap eating a green ice pop near the bulletin boards.

"Big Joe!" Andy cried.

"Yeah," Rachel said. "I saw him before. I wonder what he's doing here."

"That's funny," Andy said. "Because a while back this kid asked for four pieces of gum instead of one. Then when I gave him two, he yanked on my tail. I looked down and it was Chip Hoover."

"No kidding," Rachel said. "I wonder what they're both doing here."

"And I wonder why Mr. Hudson's not here," Andy said. "The whole reason he was in town was to come to this show. Right?"

"We better keep our eyes peeled," Rachel said. "Well, let's get back to work. You check out the booth. I'll follow Joe around and see who he meets up with."

"Check," Andy said through his mask.

About five minutes later Andy saw it: the red fishing hat.

Mr. Hudson was at R-43 and he was moving fast. Andy figured he'd make it to R-56 in a matter of minutes.

He would have liked to contact Rachel, but she was way over by the stairs.

So Andy decided to go it alone. His plan was to stay near the booth. He wanted to be close—but not so close that it looked suspicious.

As Mr. Hudson moved to R-53 Andy tensed. A kid asked him for bubble gum cards. He gave him three packs without even thinking.

Andy noticed that Mr. Hudson was carrying a little case under his arm. Suddenly an idea dawned on him: Inside that case was Grandpa's Championship ring!

Andy was so sure of it he nearly jumped out of his costume.

"Calm down, Andy," he muttered to himself as

Mr. Hudson approached R-56. Andy decided to move in closer and pretend to be looking the other way.

Suddenly there was a voice.

"Excuse me, do you have a pencil I could borrow?" the voice asked. It was Mr. Hudson.

Andy froze. What should he do? Should he try to run? Should he try to grab the guy? Should he call for help? What?

"Excuse me," Mr. Hudson said again. "Anyone home in there? Hello?"

"Hunh?" Andy said dumbly through his mask.

And then Mr. Hudson chuckled, "Oh, I'm sorry. How *could* you have a pencil with that moose costume on. It doesn't have any pockets!"

Andy nodded stiffly.

"Oh, here we go," Mr. Hudson said, reaching in his jacket pocket and pulling out a ballpoint pen.

He wrote a short message on a slip of paper. Then he placed the slip in an envelope, closed it, sealed it, and left it in the R-56 message box.

"Gotcha!" Andy thought.

Then he waited. He expected Mr. Hudson to keep on going. But he didn't. He just stood by a small railing a few feet from R-56 and wouldn't move.

"Now what?" Andy muttered to himself.

A little girl came by and asked for bubble gum. Andy was so distracted he didn't hear her.

"You're a mean Minnesota Moose," she cried. Then she nudged him. "I want my bubble gum!"

Hearing the commotion, several people came by.

"Hey look," a teenager cried. "That kid's pulling on the Moose's tail. This is hilarious!"

Andy didn't get things straightened out until Rachel arrived.

"Break it up!" she cried, giving a whole handful of bubble gum packs to the little girl.

"What's going on here?" a security guard asked.

"Everything's fine!" Rachel said in a big fake voice. Then she turned to Andy.

"How long's he been here?" she asked under her breath, motioning toward Mr. Hudson.

"About ten minutes," Andy whispered. "Since he wrote his message, he hasn't moved."

"Well, he's going right now!" Rachel said. "That security guard must've scared him off."

They watched the red fishing hat make its way to the lobby and disappear. Then they rushed to the message box. There were dozens of messages in there, but only one was in an envelope.

As Rachel tore it open, Andy felt like he was going to faint.

"Well, what does it say?" Andy asked breathlessly.

She handed it to him. The message contained only six words. It said: "I only do business in person." Then there was a phone number. And it was signed, "C. Hudson."

7 Waldo

Practice on Saturday was held early. The field had to be cleared because the Mudsharks were scheduled to play an afternoon game against the Burger House Bulls.

Andy showed up carrying a bunch of old newspapers and magazines under his arm.

"What's with the magazines and newspapers?" Marty asked him.

Andy was about to answer when he saw a strange-looking contraption approaching from left field.

"What the . . ." he cried.

It was some kind of machine—but what?

"Looks like a monster!" Luis cried.

"Looks more like a dishwasher to me," Zach quipped.

H.P. barked loudly at the machine. Then he backed away.

"It's the coach," Susan giggled, as the device came wheeling in toward the mound.

"Meet Waldo," the coach announced to the team.

"What is it?" Ernie asked.

The coach smiled. "Waldo is a pitching machine," he said. "Actually, Waldo's just an old tennis ball machine that my brother-in-law doesn't need anymore. But we're going to use Waldo as a pitching machine."

"We're gonna hit tennis balls?" Marty asked.

"That's about the size of it," the coach said. "Any volunteers? How about you, Andy?"

A few minutes later, Andy stood at the plate with a bat in his hands. He peered out at Waldo.

The machine seemed to wink back at him—or was it just Andy's imagination?

The coach turned the switch to *on*.

Waldo wheezed, sputtered, and coughed. Wheels turned, levers clanked, gears rotated, and belts squealed. Then, with a final groan, a tennis ball came spinning out toward Andy.

"Swing!" the coach cried.

Andy took a mighty rip. The ball hit him on the knee.

"How'm I supposed to hit a pitch like that?" Andy cried.

"Hmm," the coach said. "Maybe Waldo needs a lit-

tle adjusting." He took out a screwdriver and tightened Waldo's belt.

The next pitch hit Andy on the elbow.

"That smarts!" Andy said, grinning. "Good thing Waldo's only pitching tennis balls."

Several Sluggers chuckled.

The next pitch whizzed past Andy's ear.

"The point here," the coach said, "is you never know about Waldo. He could be up or down. He could be anywhere—in or out of the strike zone. Let's see you beat Waldo, Andy. Let's see you hit five pitches in a row."

"Five?" Andy cried. "I doubt if I can even hit one!"

"I'll bet you can," the coach said.

The next pitch skittered off the dirt. Andy took a huge swing at it and missed.

"This is impossible!" he cried.

"You think so?" the coach said.

Now Andy was determined to hit the next pitch—one way or another. It came in high—almost over his head. Instead of taking his usual windmill swing, Andy shortened up and punched the ball into right field.

"That's one," the coach counted.

Now Waldo fired one at Andy's belt. Again he adjusted and poked the ball toward third base.

"Two!" the coach announced.

Three pitches later Andy was still making contact. He stroked the fifth pitch on a line to left.

"Five!" the coach cried. "You did it, Andy. You beat Waldo."

Andy smiled sheepishly. "Yeah, but only because I shortened up on my swing. And they weren't all solid hits. Against a real pitcher—"

Suddenly Andy stopped.

"What?" the coach asked.

"I was just gonna say that Waldo isn't very realistic," Andy said.

"Maybe not," the coach said. "But there is one thing about Waldo that is real: *You never know what's coming.*"

"I'll say," Andy replied.

"With a good pitcher it's the same thing," the coach said. "If all they did was throw strikes, hitting would be easy. But they don't. They keep you guessing. So you have to adjust. What do you think, Andy?"

Andy grinned. "I think we should start Waldo on the mound against the Mudsharks next Saturday."

The whole team roared with laughter.

Zach came over and gave Waldo a push. "No way I'm gonna get replaced by a weird-looking pitching machine!" Zach cried. "And Robin doesn't need your help either."

Now everyone laughed even harder.

"Okay, who's next?" the coach asked. "Who else wants to give Waldo a try?"

While the coach reloaded Waldo with tennis balls, Andy made his way to the bench to get his newspapers.

After practice Rachel, Seth, Zach, and Andy sat up in

the stands watching the Mudsharks warm up for their game. H.P. curled up on Rachel's lap. Chip Hoover was there. He had an open box in his hand and he was showing it to several of his teammates.

Suddenly Andy heard Big Joe's familiar voice.

"Well, if it isn't old Windmill West," he shouted up from the field. "Hey, Windmill—still looking for your ring? I know where you can get one just like it."

"Where?" Andy shouted. Big Joe looked surprised that Andy was taking him so seriously.

"Why, that's easy, West," he said. "At the concession stand. In a box of Cracker Jacks!"

"Very funny," Andy muttered.

"Come on, let's get outta here," Seth said. "We've got to go somewhere and talk."

"About what?" Andy said.

"What do you think?" Seth asked impatiently. "The ring, of course! Don't you want to get it back?"

Five minutes later, the four were sitting in the shade of the large oak tree where they always held their meetings.

Andy held the note from Mr. Hudson in his lap.

"The way I see it," Andy said, "there's only one thing we can do. Set up a meeting with Mr. Hudson face to face. And tell him to hand it over."

"What—and call off Operation Fudgebar?" Zach groaned.

"He said he'll only do business with us in person," Andy said. "Face to face."

"Yeah," Zach said. "But as soon as he sees our faces, we're cooked. He'll ditch the ring."

"Maybe," Andy said. "He carries around this little black case. The ring's in there. I'm sure of it."

"So all we need to do," Seth said, "is get a look inside that case."

"Yeah, but how?" Zach asked.

He looked over and saw Rachel's eyes narrowing. She had stopped petting H.P.

"Don't look now, anyone," Zach said. "I think my sister's getting one of her famous ideas."

Slowly, all eyes turned to Rachel.

"Come on, tell us what it is!" Andy urged.

"Well," Rachel began, "what if we had a meeting with Mr. Hudson—and we wore the mascot costumes? I'm sure Mr. Sherman would let us borrow them."

Everyone groaned.

"Now hold on," Rachel continued. "I know it sounds weird. But suppose we were to meet him at a place where *lots* of people were wearing costumes."

"Like where?" Andy said suspiciously.

"Where do people wear costumes?" Rachel asked.

"A masquerade party?" Seth offered.

"Perfect," Rachel said. "Except, of course, there is no masquerade party till Halloween."

"Halloween!" everyone moaned.

Then suddenly Rachel's eyes lit up.

"Tuesday is the Fourth of July!" she cried.

"So?" Andy said.

"What happens on the Fourth of July?" Rachel asked.

"Fireworks?" Andy suggested.

"A barbecue?" Zach said.

"Come on!" Rachel cried. "The parade. Don't you see it? People wear costumes in the Fourth of July parade!"

"The Sluggers are supposed to *march* in that parade," Andy said. "As part of the Lotus Pines Youth Baseball League."

"So?" Rachel said. "We'll set up the meeting for after the parade. Next to one of the big floats."

"How about *our* float?" Zach suggested.

Every year Rachel and Zach's father drove a giant ice cream cone through the streets of Lotus Pines advertising the Southside Ice Cream Shop.

"Perfect," Rachel said. "Three of us will hide out inside the cone."

"Then what happens?" Andy asked.

"The Minnesota Moose comes running up," Rachel replied. "He says 'Hi, I'm David Kramer.' "

"Why doesn't he take off his costume?" Andy asked.

"You wore it yourself, Andy," Rachel said. "It's hard to get off and on. He pretends it's stuck."

"Perfect!" Zach and Seth cried.

"I don't know," Andy said.

"What?" Rachel frowned.

"I just can't see myself doing this," Andy said.

"Pretending I'm David Kramer, stuck in a moose suit."

"You don't have to," Rachel said.

"I don't?" Andy said.

"Not really," she continued. "Since he can't see our faces, any one of us can pose as the Moose. For example—what about old Clear Out?"

"Hold on a second here, folks!" Seth cried. "You think I'm—"

Rachel's eyes gleamed. "You'll be perfect," she said.

8 Moose Business

The Fourth of July was a bright, hot morning. The sidewalks were packed with people. Flags flew and floats lined the streets. Everyone was waiting for the parade to start.

The floats included the giant ice cream cone, an immense shoe, and a huge pizza. There were marching bands, inflated cartoon characters, Boy Scouts and Girl Scouts, horses, Youth Baseball Leaguers, and a baby pig named Ed.

The parade was scheduled to depart from the Morgan Street Firehouse at ten o'clock sharp. From there it would turn up Plum Creek Road to Main Street, where it would officially end at 11:30 A.M. Afterward, all the floats would park in the town square in front of the city hall.

The Southside Sluggers assembled in front of the

firehouse with the other Youth Baseball League teams. They were lined up right behind the Mudsharks. Luis was carrying the team banner. Behind him, in two neat rows, were the rest of the Sluggers.

"Okay, everyone, let's go!" the parade leader cried.

As the parade started to move, Rachel looked at Seth. The plan was set. They would meet Mr. Hudson at 11:45 A.M. at the ice-cream cone float. The moose costume was hidden safely under the counter at the Southside Ice Cream Shop, just a few doors down from City Hall.

For a second, everyone was pressed close together. In all the noise and confusion Rachel thought she overheard someone say something about a Championship ring. She looked up and saw Chip Hoover.

Then the music started and she couldn't hear a thing.

They marched for over an hour. The band played patriotic songs. Baton twirlers, clowns, and acrobats put on a show. The horses trotted while Ed the baby pig scooted around on a leash.

By the time they reached the town square, everyone was worn out.

"Parading is hard work," Andy said. "My feet are killing me."

"Feet," Zach said. "My pitching arm's sore from waving so much. And my jaw hurts from smiling."

As the parade came to an end, everyone cheered.

"Let's go!" Seth said.

The four Sluggers rushed to the ice cream shop. Seth wriggled into his moose costume while the others watched Mr. Langlin park the float near a bench.

"Hi, Dad," Rachel said. "Want us to watch the float for you?"

"Sure," Mr. Langlin said with a smile.

A small door opened at the bottom of the cone. Out crawled Gregg, a teenager who worked at the shop. He'd been riding in the cone with his head sticking out the top.

"Hi, Rach," he said.

When Gregg was gone, Rachel motioned for Zach and Andy. Then she opened the little door and the three of them crawled inside the cone.

"This is great," Rachel said. "Just like the Trojan Horse."

"The *what* horse?" Zach asked.

"Trojan," Rachel said. "It's an old story. The ancient Greeks hid inside a huge wooden horse to fool their enemy."

"Did they fool them?" Andy asked.

"I think so," Rachel said. "I can't remember."

"I'm squished!" Zach cried. "Can you see anything?"

"Here comes the Moose," Rachel said.

Seth walked up in his moose suit and gave a knock.

"Well?" he said.

"Nothing yet," Rachel told him. "Oh, wait—here he comes! Quick—down, everyone!"

A minute later a man wearing a red fishing hat came walking up to Seth.

"Mr. Kramer?" Mr. Hudson said. The two shook hands.

"Sorry about this moose suit," Seth said. "I was wearing it in the parade."

"Funny," Mr. Hudson said. "I didn't see you in the parade. I *did* see you somewhere, though."

"I was back with the horses," Seth said. He began struggling with his moose mask.

"Hey—can I give you a hand with that suit?" Mr. Hudson asked.

"Oh, no, no, no," Seth said. "Very tricky suit. One wrong move and you rip the whole thing. It's always like this. Why don't I just leave it on and we'll get down to business?"

Mr. Hudson looked at the moose costume for a few seconds and then laughed loudly.

"Sorry," he said, trying to control his laughter. "I've never done business with a moose before."

Mr. Hudson then sat down on the bench and got out his little black case. Seth held his breath and waited.

Then suddenly there was a cough from inside the cone. To cover it up, Seth started coughing.

"You okay?" Mr. Hudson asked.

"I'll be fine," Seth rasped. "Just a little hard to breathe inside this mask."

"Now," Mr. Hudson said. "You said you were interested in a nineteen-fifties Championship ring from a local semipro league.

"Did I?" Seth asked. "Oh, right. Of course."

"Well, would you like to see it?" Mr. Hudson asked.

Seth looked over at the cone.

"That depends," he said nervously.

"On what?" Mr. Hudson asked.

There was another cough.

"On, uh, whether you've got it," he said.

"Oh, I've got it all right," Mr. Hudson said, tapping the side of his little black case. "The question is, Mr. Kramer—what do *you* have?"

"Me?" Seth said. Mr. Hudson's eyes seemed to be burning a hole right through his moose mask.

"Yes, you," Mr. Hudson said. "Are you sure you can't let me help you with that mask, Mr. Kramer? It looks awfully uncomfortable in there."

"I'm fine," Seth said nervously. "Now, you were saying?"

"I was asking," Mr. Hudson said, "if you are really the person you say you are."

"Of course I am!" Seth insisted.

Suddenly there was a sneeze. There was no doubt about it this time. It came from inside the cone.

Mr. Hudson smiled.

Inside his mask Seth smiled back.

"Now I remember where I saw you," Mr. Hudson said. "The memorabilia show. Last Wednesday. I asked you for a pencil, remember?"

"You did?" Seth croaked. "Oh, right. Of course. The pencil. How could I forget?"

There was another sneeze. Mr. Hudson shook his head. Seth pulled his moose antlers down over his eyes.

"Okay, the game's up," Mr. Hudson said. "Whoever you are, you can come out from inside that cone now."

Suddenly Seth stood up and tore off his mask.

"They'll come out," he cried, "if you'll show us the Championship rings you have in that box!"

"With pleasure!" Mr. Hudson replied.

And with that he opened the case. Meanwhile, Rachel, Zach, and Andy came tumbling out of the cone, coughing and sneezing.

"Andy!" Mr. Hudson cried. "What the—"

Andy scrambled over to get a look inside the case. There were over twenty rings inside, arranged by year from the 1950s up to the 1970s.

"Aha!" Seth cried. "Look, Andy—nineteen-fifty-four!"

Sure enough, it was a 1954 Championship ring. But when Andy turned it over to look for the inscription, there was nothing there!

"That's not my ring!" Andy cried.

"Of course not!" Mr. Hudson said. "Why would you think it was your ring?"

"Then you didn't—" Andy began.

"I didn't *what*?" Mr. Hudson demanded.

"What Andy's trying to say here, Mr. Hudson, is that you didn't steal his ring," Rachel said.

Mr. Hudson shook his head slowly and smiled.

"So that's what this is all about," he said.

It took them almost a half an hour to explain the whole thing.

It turned out that Mr. Hudson's 1954 ring had belonged to another player on Ike Rudolph's team. In fact, it was the ring given to the team's star pitcher.

"What a letdown," Andy said. "I'm glad you're not a crook, Mr. Hudson. But now it means my ring is gone."

"I understand," Mr. Hudson replied. "Do you have any other idea about who might have taken the ring?"

The Sluggers shook their heads.

"Do you?" Rachel asked.

"You know, come to think of it," Mr. Hudson mused, "there was something. Two days ago I got a message from a boy who'd seen my sign at the memorabilia show asking for Championship rings."

"What did it say?" Seth asked.

Mr. Hudson took out his wallet and began searching through slips of paper.

"Well, he was just a boy," Mr. Hudson said. "But he definitely said something about selling a Championship ring. Oh, here's his number. Hoover was his name. Chip Hoover. Does that ring any bells?"

At the plate the next day, in the top of the second against the Rocket Raiders, all Andy could think about was Chip Hoover.

Matt Montoya was pitching. With a one and one count, in came a fastball that Andy just looked at.

"Stee-rike two!" the umpire barked.

Chip Hoover! Andy thought. *He must have grabbed the ring during that play at the plate. When I was still on the ground.*

In came another pitch.

"Ball!" the umpire snarled.

Now it was coming clear, Andy thought. *The way Chip was acting—like it was a big joke.*

The next pitch was high and outside.

"Ball!" came the umpire's yell.

Andy dropped his bat and slowly trotted toward first base. When he got there, Biff Morgan, the first baseman, was smiling. The umpire waved for Andy to come back.

"What's goin' on?" Andy asked.

Biff chuckled. "That was ball three, pal. You need *four* balls for a walk. Remember?"

Andy dashed back to home plate and picked up his bat.

"Pay attention, son!" the umpire barked.

But by the time the next pitch came in, Andy was thinking again—about the plan for catching Chip.

Could they really trust Mr. Hudson? he wondered.

When the next pitch came in, Andy somehow managed to swing. It was not a "swing from the heart." It was more like the little punch-swings he took when Waldo was pitching. But he did get the bat on the ball.

And it sailed up the middle for a base hit.

The Sluggers were already behind, 6–1, to the powerful Raiders team. But, when Ernie and Zach followed Andy with hits, they threatened to make a game of it. Then Rachel struck out, and Susan forced Andy out at the plate. Two outs. But the bases were still loaded.

"Come on!" Andy cried from the bench.

Clear Out Bradigan promptly crushed one into deep left center. The ball bounced just before the fence, where a bare hand reached over and caught it.

Some spectator had interfered with the play!

"Ground-rule double!" the umpire cried.

"Double!" Zach cried. "He could've gotten at least a triple on that hit. Or even a grand-slam homer. What a gyp!"

"Who was that who grabbed the ball out there, anyway?" Rachel asked. She walked to the edge of the bench with H.P. at her side.

"Look!" Andy said. "It was Big Joe! What's *he* doing here?"

"Causing trouble as usual," Rachel said. "Probably just wants to make sure we don't pull any big upsets."

But something didn't seem right. Ever since he had lost the ring, Andy always seemed to be running into two people—Chip Hoover and Big Joe. Somehow, he felt, it meant something. But what?

When Marty flied out to end the inning, Big Joe's interference seemed huge. Without his big hand getting in the way, four runs might have scored, making it 6–5.

As it was, the Sluggers took the field down 6–3.

Robin Hayes came in to pitch in the fourth inning. And the Raiders quickly jumped to a 9–3 lead. The Sluggers then came back in the top of the fifth.

With one out, Michelle sliced a triple down the right-field line, making the score 9–5.

Then Luis walked. Andy realized that it was up to him to keep the rally alive. He tried to concentrate. Andy tried to force Big Joe, Chip Hoover, Mr. Hudson, even Grandpa's ring out of his thoughts.

Andy had to think only about the game. It was him against the pitcher. Now Andy suddenly felt that he knew what "swing from the heart" really meant. It meant, No matter what—you had to go for it. Even if you failed.

He saw what happened last time he was up. Sure, he got a hit. But because he didn't truly swing from the heart, it wasn't the big hit he was looking for.

This time it would be different. A homer here would put the Sluggers ahead of the mighty Rocket Raiders!

With a two-ball, two-strike count, Andy got his pitch. He swung so hard it almost hurt. And the ball went flying.

Straight up.

It took about ten seconds for it to come down—right in the catcher's mitt.

"Gee, that thing was high," the catcher said. "I almost got dizzy waiting for it."

Andy slammed his bat on the ground. The Sluggers never got any closer and lost the game, 12–5.

"Oh, well, back to the drawing board," Marty said, as the team left the field. "Sooner or later we're gonna win one of these games against a top team. Don't you think, Andy?"

Andy stared at the ground. "I don't know," he said. "Maybe that's our problem."

"What?" Marty said.

"Maybe we're not ready to win the big games yet," Andy replied.

9 Donut Holes

Andy usually tried to avoid things like long division. But the following evening he sat in his room with an old local newspaper in his lap, dividing 692 hits by 2,683 at bats.

The newspaper said that Ike Rudolph had finished his semipro career with a total of 692 hits in 2,683 times at bat. No matter how many times Andy divided the two numbers, he came up with the same thing. His grandpa only had a .258 career batting average.

Something was wrong.

Fifty-seven home runs sounded like a lot. But Andy suddenly realized that it took Ike eight years to hit those homers. That was only about seven home runs a season.

Something was definitely wrong!

Andy looked at the picture in the old newspaper. The caption underneath read: "Ike 'The Rock' Rudolph."

Maybe "The Rock" wasn't such a power hitter after all, Andy thought. *Or maybe he only hit homers when the team really needed them. Like that famous blast in the fourth game of the Championship Series.*

Suddenly there was a knock at his door.

"Andy," Mrs. West said excitedly. "I met Linda Pollack from the *Lotus Times* at the grocery. I was talking to her about your grandpa's ring. And she wants to do an article about your grandpa and the ring for the newspaper! Isn't that great?"

"Uh-huh," Andy said, trying to sound excited.

"Anyway," she added, "I told Linda she could meet you at your game on Saturday. They want to take a picture of you and the ring for the paper!"

Before Andy could say anything, the doorbell rang. It was Rachel and Seth.

"It's all set," Rachel told him.

Andy looked down.

"What's wrong?" Rachel asked.

"Nothing," Andy sighed. "What's all set?"

"Operation Fudge-Burger," Seth said.

"Fudge-Burger?" Andy groaned.

"Mr. Hudson's going to meet with Chip Hoover at Burger House," Seth said. "Get it? Fudge Burger."

"I get it," Andy said in a sad, flat voice. "When do they meet?"

Rachel looked at her watch. "In about thirty minutes," she said. "We better get over there."

"Why Burger House?" Andy asked.

"'Cause it's a big noisy place where we can stand nearby without being noticed," Rachel said.

"What do we do there?" Andy asked, still unclear about the plan.

"Just stay in the background," Seth said. "And wait for the signal from Mr. Hudson. Then we'll nab Chip."

Burger House was a great place. It had a whole family of house burgers, from the giant Big House Special to the tiny Itty-Bitty House Burger. It also had game rooms, a giant-screen TV, and the best homestyle french fries in the county.

Zach was already there, waiting for them. He was sitting at a back table with his feet up, watching a baseball game on the big-screen TV.

"This is the life," he said, offering Andy a french fry. "You want one?"

"I'm not hungry," Andy said. "Where's Mr. Hudson?"

Zach pointed to a table in the front. "Over there," he said. "But you can't see him from here."

"Who's ahead?" Seth asked, pointing to the TV.

"I think Oakland's down by two," Zach said. "But they have a runner on base and their best hitter's coming to bat."

The four Sluggers looked up at the figure on the screen. He was standing in the on-deck circle, swinging a bat. He took one more warm-up swing, then pulled the heavy metal "donut" ring off the end of his bat and walked to the plate.

Rachel, Zach, and Seth sat there silently staring at the TV, munching french fries.

"I hate to break this up," Andy said. "But Mr. Hudson just hung his hat on the post. Isn't that the signal?"

"You bet it is," Seth said. "Let's get over there."

The four Sluggers crept past the video room to a hallway next to the kitchen. From there, they were just out of sight of Mr. Hudson's table. The four stood in a line against the wall, Rachel in front. She was the only one who could see very well.

"What's he saying?" Andy asked her.

"Hold your horses," Rachel said. "They just shook hands. Now Chip's taking off his jacket."

She stood silently for a moment and tried to listen.

"What's he saying?" Andy asked again.

"I can't tell," Rachel said. "Something about a ring, I think. Now they're looking up at the TV. Wait! Oh, no!"

"What's wrong?" Andy shrieked.

"I knew it!" Rachel moaned.

"Knew *what*?" Andy cried frantically.

"The Oakland batter," Rachel said. "He hit a home run. I knew they never should've pitched to him."

"Let me up there," Andy said, pushing his way forward. "You're making me too nervous."

"You stay back," Seth said. He pulled Andy back behind the wall.

"Now what?" Andy asked, still on edge.

Rachel pushed her head forward so she could see. "Mr. Hudson took out his little black case," she said.

"What about Chip?" Andy asked.

"He's got his box," Rachel said.

"This is it!" Seth cried.

"Not quite," Rachel said. "Hold on. Something's wrong here."

"What? What is it?" Andy demanded.

"Mr. Hudson's laughing," Rachel said.

"*Laughing?*" Andy said. "Why's he laughing?"

"I don't know," Rachel admitted.

"This is serious business," Andy moaned. "We'll never get my ring back this way. What's happening now?"

"Chip's laughing too," Rachel said.

"What're they laughing about?" Andy cried. He was squeezing Zach's arm so tight it was turning white.

"Hey, watch it," Zach said. "That hurts!"

"I'm goin' out there!" Andy whispered in an intense voice.

"You can't," Rachel said. "Wait. Now Chip's starting to open the box. He's gonna show what's inside and—"

"Outta my way," Andy snapped. "I'm gonna see for myself what's in that box."

When Andy appeared at the table, Chip gave him a big, friendly smile.

"West," he said. "Grab a seat. You look starved. Want some fries?"

Andy pushed him away.

"Cut the funny stuff, Chip," Andy snapped. "Where's the Championship ring?"

Now both Chip and Mr. Hudson started laughing.

"What?" Andy said. Then his eyes narrowed. "Oh, I see. You two are in on this together, aren't you?"

He made a grab for Chip's box. What rolled out was a ring, all right. But it was so big, it would have fit around Andy's arm.

"What's this?" Andy groaned. "You call this a Championship ring?"

"That's exactly what it is," Mr. Hudson said, still giggling a bit.

"But what—" Andy began.

"It's a batting ring," Chip said. "You know, a donut. Like the kind they use in the on-deck circle. To weight down their bats during warm-up swings. My uncle got it from the semipro league Championship Series last year. Honest!"

Andy just stood there.

"You mean to tell me—" he began again.

"It's all a mix-up," Mr. Hudson said. "When Chip saw my sign about semipro Championship rings he thought maybe I'd be interested in one of these."

"A donut?" Andy said, flinging his arms into the air.

"Well it *is* a ring," Chip said. "And it was in the semipro Championship Series. Maybe it's not as good as your ring. But I figure it must be worth something."

Andy picked up the donut. It was much heavier than it looked.

"You mean to tell me that this thing is the Championship ring you wanted to sell?" Andy asked.

Mr. Hudson suddenly felt Andy's disappointment. "I'm sorry, Andy," he said. "It was all just a mistake."

"Well, now what am I supposed to do?" Andy asked.

Hot tears were beginning to well up in his eyes. He turned and walked back behind the wall toward Rachel.

"Well?" she asked.

But Andy didn't answer. He just kept on walking, down the hallway, past the counter, out into the cool, late afternoon air.

Half an hour later, the four friends were sitting on the steps leading to the Langlins' front porch.

"You don't understand," Andy said. "I need the ring by Saturday. After our game against the Mudsharks, they're going to take a picture of me and the ring for the newspaper."

"That just means we better get moving," Zach said.

"Get *moving*?" Andy snapped. "On what? We're running out of suspects!"

"Well," Seth said. "There's still Big Joe Jones. He had the chance to grab the ring during the collision. And he really seemed to want your grandfather's ring."

"I guess that makes him the one we're after," Zach said.

"It's possible," Rachel said. "But how do we prove it? How do we find out for sure that Joe took the ring?"

"Hmm," Seth said. "That's a tough one to figure out."

The four of them sat there. Rachel doodled in her notebook. Zach blew bubbles. Seth bounced a ball on the steps. And Andy stared off into space.

"Enough!" Zach finally said. "It's getting late."

"And we're getting nowhere," Seth added.

"You know what I'm thinking," Andy said sadly. "Maybe Big Joe didn't steal the ring. I mean, we're really just guessing."

"Then who did?" Zach asked. "The man in the moon?"

"Maybe," Andy sighed, close to tears. "Or maybe no one. Maybe I just lost it somehow. The trouble is, wherever I lost it, it's not there anymore."

"If only we had some kind of time machine," Zach said. "Then we could go back in time to the exact moment Big Joe slid into home."

"What good would that do?" Seth asked. "Everything happened too fast. We still might not figure out what really happened."

"We'd just turn the time machine on Slow Motion," Zach said. "With everything slowed down, we could tell exactly where the ring went."

"Wait a second," Rachel said. "That's a great idea."

"Of course it's a great idea," Zach said. "Too bad time machines don't exist."

"But they *do* exist," Rachel said. "Quick, Zach. Go inside and get the phone book."

"You're going to make a *time machine* out of a *phone book*?" Zach cried. "This I gotta see!"

10 Slow Motion

Andy peeked out from under the grandstand at Bloom Field. Next to him sat Rachel, Seth, and Zach. Rachel held H.P. close to keep him quiet. It was Saturday morning. In two hours the Sluggers would have their big rematch against the Mudsharks.

"I don't see why we're here so early," Zach said. "What exactly did that letter ask the Mudsharks to do?"

Rachel held up the letter she'd sent out to all the Mudsharks. It was typed on the family computer. And the copies had been run off on her father's copying machine.

"'Dear Mudshark,'" Rachel read. "'As you may know, Andy West is offering a twenty-five dollar

reward for the nineteen-fifty-four semipro Championship ring he lost near home plate in our last game. If
you want to help find it, please show up for Saturday's
game at Bloom Field *thirty minutes early*.' "

It was signed, "Your arch-rivals, The Southside
Sluggers. P.S. We're going to *beat* you guys!"

"So that's why you needed the phone book," Zach
said. "To get the addresses of all the Mudsharks. But I
still don't see why we're here now. The game doesn't
start for two whole hours."

"To see if Big Joe shows up earlier than everybody
else," Rachel said. "Let's see how much he wants to
find that ring."

"That would be sort of cheating," Zach said. "He'd
be getting a big jump on everybody else."

Seth nodded. "Yup, it would kind of be cheating the
other kids. But if he cheats, at least we'll know that Big
Joe's honest."

"Huh?" Zach said. "Well, what if he doesn't cheat?"

"Then he's dishonest," Seth said. "Maybe."

Zach blew several nervous bubbles. "Is it just me,"
he said, "or is this sort of confusing?"

"Look," Seth said. "What if Big Joe stole the ring?"

"Then he *won't* come looking for it," Andy said.
"At least not *this* early."

"Correct," Seth said. "Why won't he?"

"Oh, I get it," Zach said. "'Cause he already *has* it.
And if he *didn't* steal the ring . . ."

"Then we're betting he'll cheat and come early to

look for it," Rachel said. "But he'll never find it anyway. We all searched the area around home plate. The ring is definitely not there."

"But, if Joe *did* take the ring," added Seth, "he might come here early to hide it. Then he could pretend to find it later and collect the reward. He wouldn't be able to show off a hot ring anyhow."

"We have that covered too," Rachel replied. "If he comes early to hide the ring, we'll be here to nab him."

"But what about the *slow-motion replay*?" Zach said. "You think that will give us a clue to what *did* happen to the ring?"

"That's later," Rachel said. "Right now, we want to see if Big Joe is still our top suspect. Hey, who's that coming?"

They heard voices near third base.

"It's Big Joe and his older brother!" Andy whispered. "I guess this means Joe doesn't have the ring."

"Or he's here to hide it," challenged Seth.

"What're they saying?" Zach asked.

Rachel poked her head out between the second and third row of grandstand benches and listened.

"Ha!" she cried. "They're talking about the reward."

"Yeah," Seth reported. "They said they'll search every inch of the home plate area if they have to. They want that reward!"

"Let 'em search," Zach snapped. "Let 'em knock themselves out. Greedy guys!"

"Maybe they are greedy," Andy said. "But they're also innocent."

"True," Seth said. "Now we know for sure. Big Joe didn't steal the ring."

"Then who did?" Andy moaned, throwing his glove to the ground.

Rachel shook her head. "Maybe no one," she said.

A half hour before game time, both teams started to show up. When everyone was there, Rachel rolled up her notebook like a megaphone and said, "Welcome, Mudsharks, to the First-Ever Andy West Lost Championship Ring Slow-Motion Replay."

She looked to acknowledge the players' whistles, shouts, and clapping.

"Some of you may ask, 'What's this all about?' The answer is: It's too complicated to explain."

Several of the kids laughed and yelled comments.

"To be brief," Rachel said, "it goes like this: Andy lost his ring on that big final play at the plate last game. We hope, if we reenact that play in slow motion, that we can learn what happened to the ring. Okay? Please take your places, everybody."

Players on both teams were muttering to each other. But nobody seemed to be refusing to help.

"Hey, Andy," Rachel yelled. "Don't forget Zach's plastic ring."

Andy slipped Zach's old toy decoder ring on his finger. It fit loosely like his grandpa's ring. So it made a good substitute for the lost Championship ring.

"Check," Andy said. "I've got Zach's ring on."

The Sluggers took their positions on the field. Big Joe trotted to second as a base runner. Mike Moran stood up at the plate to bat, just as before. Even Mr. Joyner, the umpire, came early. He put on his mask and crouched behind the plate.

"Go!" Rachel yelled from right field. "Remember, everyone—this is in *slow motion*."

Zach took a ridiculously slow windup before he lobbed in the pitch. Mike then took a huge "slow-mo" hack at the pitch and missed.

"C'mon, Mike!" Rachel yelled. "Hit the ball, will ya!"

"I can't hit in slow motion!" Mike shot back.

Someone on the sideline called out, "He can't hit in *any* motion!"

Rachel thought it over for a moment. Then she told Mike to go ahead and swing normally. This time Mike somehow managed to hit the ball. A weak fly ball went spinning to left.

"Okay, start the play in slow motion, everyone!" Rachel cried.

Just then, Linda Pollack from the *Lotus Times* showed up with Mrs. West. She looked out at the field. She didn't understand what she was seeing. A bunch of kids were playing baseball *at the wrong speed*.

"What's going on here?" she cried.

In slow motion, Seth charged the ball from the outfield. Meanwhile, Big Joe slowly moved toward third as if he were running underwater.

Mr. Hudson was also at the field. He stood near H.P. on the sidelines.

Meanwhile, Big Joe inched his way around third and headed for home. It was just as before—Andy, the ball, and Big Joe were all going to collide at the same exact time.

The umpire slowly crouched and leaned gradually into position.

Andy flung off his mask with his right hand. The loosely fitting plastic decoder ring flew into the air. It bounced off the crouching umpire's arm before landing on the ground by his feet.

A split second later, Big Joe took a long, easy slide. Andy slowly snared the ball as it floated in. The two collided and the dust flew lazily into the air. The umpire leaned *way* forward and baseballs rolled out of his jacket pocket.

"*Cut!*" yelled Rachel, just like a movie director. "Okay, that was perfect, everyone. Thanks very much. You can go back to what you were doing. I particularly want to thank *you*, Mr. Joyner.

"What about the reward?" Mike Moran yelled, walking away, still in slow motion.

"Find the ring," Rachel called after him.

Only Andy stayed where he was, staring at the plastic ring on the ground.

"Well?" Rachel said, when she reached home plate. "Learn anything new from this?"

"The ring flew off when I whipped off my mask," Andy said.

"Well, I think there might be something else that can help us," said Rachel, already deep in thought. "Let me work on it."

But Andy was already convinced that he would never see his Championship ring again. He felt a terrible sinking feeling in his stomach.

Andy also felt a little sick about having to face Ken Allan. He was the Mudsharks' top pitcher. And there was nothing slow motion about the way Ken was zinging them in today. In warm-ups, Ken was rearing back and just firing the ball across the plate.

While Andy was glaring out at Ken from the sideline, Mr. Hudson came over and handed Andy an old *Lotus Times* clipping dated October 7, 1954. Andy had been searching for this article. It was an in-depth article about game four of the 1954 semipro league Championship Series.

Finally, Andy would be able to read about Ike's big home run. The way he creamed one into the stands to win a close game for the Lotus Pines Hawks. Except it hadn't happened that way.

Actually, it had been a phony bunt play. Andy couldn't believe it. Ike Rudolph, "The Rock," the power hitter, faked a bunt in the Championship Series with the game on the line!

Two runners were on base. The other team saw Ike turn to face the pitcher with his bat out front, ready for the bunt. The infield instantly took three steps in.

But Ike crossed them up. Instead of bunting, he just guided the ball over third base. It rolled all the way to the left-field corner.

The left fielder had been moving in to back up the bunt. When the ball sailed by him, he had to reverse gears and chase it down. The fleet-footed Ike just kept running until he crossed home plate.

This was Ike's famous game-winning home run! Not a four-hundred-foot blast, but a little floater that caught the other team going the wrong way.

In the top half of the first inning, three Mudshark ground balls caught the Sluggers' infield moving the wrong way. The Mudsharks wound up with three singles and a 1–0 lead.

Then, in the bottom of the first, Ken Allan took over. The Mudsharks pitcher mowed down the Sluggers' leadoff batters. Rachel popped up to the catcher. Susan Stein struck out. And even Seth could only manage an easy-out grounder to first base.

Luckily, Robin Hayes started to settle down in the top of the second inning. The Southside Sluggers relief pitcher struck out both Chip and Billy Butler before giving up a bloop single. She then closed out the Mudsharks' turn at bat by catching a pop-up back to the pitcher's mound. She was making the most of a rare opportunity to start.

The pitcher's duel continued into the bottom of the second inning. Ken forced Marty to ground out. He then struck out Michelle on three straight pitches. But Luis reached second base on a throwing error by the Mudsharks shortstop and a catching error by the player on first.

Andy now came to bat with two outs and a runner on second base. It was the closest thing to a scoring opportunity for the Sluggers so far. He felt the pressure to *make something happen.*

After two windmill swings at two hard fastballs, Andy had two strikes. This wasn't working! He was swinging more from the knot in his stomach than from his heart.

Andy backed out of the batter's box. It was finally starting to sink in. Ike Rudolph was no power hitter! After the game the reporters had asked Ike whether his big hit was planned — or just an accident.

"You just swing from the heart," Ike had told them, "and see what happens. That's all you can ever do. Swing from the heart."

As Ken wound up for his next pitch, Andy tried to get in touch with his feelings. *In my heart,* he thought, *what do I really feel I should do?*

Andy answered the question by trying to square up and bunt the next pitch. Just the way Grandpa Ike might have done it.

"Strike three!" the umpire barked, as Andy missed the ball.

"Hey, everyone, Windmill West can even strike out bunting!" Big Joe jeered from his position at third base.

Andy felt a hot lump rise in his throat. He had made a mistake! He had tried to do it Ike's way. He didn't swing from his *own* heart. But at least he hadn't just slashed out at the ball like an unthinking *windmill*.

By the middle of the fourth inning, the score was still 1–0. Zach came in to pitch the top of the fourth and looked brilliant. Ken Allan was looking just as good. The game was so close that it got Andy's mind off the ring for a while. But that ended when Zach and Rachel sat down next to him on the bench.

"I'm going over the suspect list," Rachel said.

Rachel went through each suspect. Mr. Hudson was out. Chip was out. And now Big Joe was out too.

Andy shook his head. "It's no use," he said. "Too bad we didn't learn anything from that slow-motion replay."

Rachel bit her lip as she watched Seth bat. "You know," she said. "There was something wrong about that replay of the collision. It was good, but it wasn't perfect."

"What?" Zach said. "The ball came in. Big Joe came in. The ring came off. End of story. What did you expect to see, anyway?"

"More," Rachel said. "I thought the toy ring would land in a more hidden kind of place. I thought it would *fall* some place more special."

"The only things I saw *falling* were those baseballs out of the umpire's jacket pocket," Zach said.

Suddenly, Rachel got that look in her eye.

"That's it!" she said. "I think you hit on something there."

"I did?" Zach said. "You think the lost ring has something to do with those baseballs?"

"Not *only* the baseballs," Rachel cried. "It also has to do with the umpire's big jacket pocket. Both times that jacket pocket flapped *wide open* and baseballs fell out."

"So?" Andy asked excitedly. "What are you telling us?"

"I'm *telling you* that after the big collision in the Mudsharks game, your ring could have sailed off your finger and into the open jacket pocket of the umpire."

"Yeah?" replied Andy, still thinking it over. "Well, let's go check Mr. Joyner's pocket right now!"

"Wait!" yelled Zach. "If Andy's ring fell into the umpire's pocket after the first collision, then why didn't my toy ring land in the same pocket during the slow-motion replay?"

"It's simple, little brother," said Rachel. "Your plastic ring bounced off the umpire's arm in the replay. That's pretty close to the jacket pocket. And the toy ring isn't as heavy as Andy's real Championship ring. Therefore, it wouldn't fly off in the exact same way or fly the exact same distance."

"It makes sense," Andy said. "I think you're right. When I get back to my catcher's position, I'm going to ask Mr. Joyner to check his pocket."

After the Sluggers went down in order again, Andy grabbed his catcher's gear. He then dashed to the plate to question the umpire. Mr. Joyner listened carefully to Andy's explanation.

"Wow!" the umpire said. "You could be right!"

Then he reached into his pocket and shook his head.

"Sorry," Mr. Joyner said. "No Championship ring in here. If what you said is right, then the ring should be in this pocket. Better come up with a new solution."

Zach continued to handle the Mudshark batters until the sixth and final inning. Then, with one out, he threw a hanger to Big Joe. The ball exploded off Joe's bat and flew over the center-field fence. The Mudsharks now had a solid 2–0 lead.

Andy felt somewhat desperate and emotional when he came up for the Sluggers' last licks. Rachel was batting first. So far, the Sluggers had managed only two scratch singles all day.

"Come on, swing from the heart!" Andy cried, still fixed on following Grandpa Ike's advice.

Rachel took two quick strikes. Then she shortened up her swing and lashed a low shot to right center for a double. H.P. began to run back and forth in front of the Sluggers' bench.

"Way to adjust!" Andy cried from the bench.

Andy could sense how Rachel had reacted *naturally* to the situation. That was *swinging from the heart*. He was starting to not only *think* about Ike's words. But to really *feel* them.

When Susan and Seth followed with singles to score

Rachel, it looked like the Sluggers were going to come roaring back for the win. But then Ken Allan bore down and struck out Marty and Michelle. When Luis popped up, Andy thought the game was over. However, it fell in for a lucky single when two Mudsharks collided.

The score was still 2–1 with two outs as Andy came to the plate. But now the bases were loaded and the pressure was really on.

In the past, Andy would have gotten all excited. He would have swung too hard and struck out. But this time he had a plan.

Andy would wait for his pitch. Then he would really try to swing from the heart. *His* heart this time! Not from what he imagined would be in Grandpa Ike's heart. If something good happened, fine. If he hit into an out, he would at least know he had tried his best.

Andy's new, calm approach to hitting was seriously tested. Ken Allan made four great pitches in a row. Two found the outside corner of the plate and two just missed. Now, with a two-ball, two-strike count, Andy had to really concentrate. He had to find his own comfortable, *natural* groove.

In came Ken's hottest fastball—right over the corner of the plate. Andy thought about mashing it. But he knew, just *felt*, that it was too good. So he reached out and tapped it foul.

Ken glared at him from the mound.

"Come on, Windmill!" Big Joe called. "You can swing harder than that!"

Andy calmly set himself. The next pitch was an inside change-up. Again, Andy felt like ripping it. But he was jammed and settled for another foul ball.

"Let's go, West!" Joe cried. "What're you afraid of?"

Ken Allan threw in three more beauties — and Andy fouled off each one. Now Ken was getting nervous. And maybe a bit tired. Even Big Joe's razzing seemed a little weak. Andy was wearing them down.

"Come on," Rachel called from the bench. "Stay with it!"

Andy smiled. Now he knew he had them.

"I'm a rock," he muttered to himself. "Just like Ike 'The Rock' Rudolph."

Suddenly, Andy understood what that nickname really meant. It meant someone who couldn't be moved. Someone who stayed with it, and with his own feelings, no matter what.

Finally, Ken's tenth pitch was a fastball that Andy knew he could hit. Even so, he didn't just swing wildly at it.

Everything happened so smoothly that it felt like slow motion. The pitch came in right down the middle of the plate. Andy took a fluid, level, relaxed swing. Crack! A solid line drive rocketed out to left center field.

Andy felt his heart leap as he rounded first base. He

looked up and spotted a glint of something small and white fly into the air. Then he glimpsed Susan cross the plate with the tying run. And Seth slid in, feet first, for the winning run a moment later.

"*Safe!*" the umpire bawled.

Andy pulled up at second and broke into a big grin. Seconds later he got mobbed by his teammates. Luis, Marty, and Susan pounded him on the back—and H.P. jumped up and down by his feet.

"We beat the Mudsharks!" Luis shouted.

"We finally won a big one!" Marty cried. "We beat our arch-rivals in a close game."

Rachel gave Andy a big hug.

"Nice rip, Windmill," she said. "And wait until you see your prize!"

A moment later Andy turned and saw Seth standing next to him with the umpire.

"I think Rachel, Mr. Joyner, and I just figured out where your Championship ring is," Seth said.

11 Swing from the Heart

"A *dry cleaner's* ticket?" Andy gasped. He'd just finished telling Ms. Pollack that he'd be right back to take the picture for the *Lotus Times*.

"Where'd you find it?" Zach chimed in.

"On the ground when I slid in with the winning run," Seth said, pointing to the umpire. "It fell out of Mr. Joyner's pocket."

"So?" Andy said. "What does all this have to do with my ring?"

"It got me thinking," Seth said. "I noticed Mr. Joyner's wearing his watch today. Last game I didn't notice it. Then I thought: *He's wearing a different jacket today, with shorter sleeves. That's why I noticed his watch. And that's also why we couldn't find the ring in his pocket. He's wearing a different jacket, with shorter sleeves!"*

"Is it true?" Rachel asked the umpire.

Mr. Joyner nodded.

"You're a genius, Clear Out," Rachel cried.

"So where's the other jacket?" Andy said.

"That's just it," Seth said. "The laundry ticket. *The long-sleeved jacket's at the cleaner's!"*

"I forgot," Mr. Joyner said. "After the game, I tossed my jacket into the car trunk. Then I went to dinner. On my way home, I dropped my jacket at Martin's Twenty-Four-Hour Cleaners."

"How many jackets do you have?" Rachel asked.

"Three," Mr. Joyner said. "The one with the longer sleeves is at the cleaners. I got this jacket from one of the umpires who left last year. And I have an older jacket that I keep in my car trunk for a spare."

"How do you tell them apart without measuring them against each other or trying them on?" Rachel asked.

"The one with the longer sleeves has a white label," Mr. Joyner said. "The other two have blue labels."

"Do you think the one at the cleaner's could have the ring in its pocket?" Rachel asked.

The umpire scratched his chin. "It's possible," he said. "The pocket is so big! Something's always flying in or out of it. And I was wearing the longer-sleeved jacket that day. I remember that!"

Rachel looked at Seth. Seth looked at Andy.

"What're we waitin' for?" Andy cried. "Let's go!"

"Where?" Zach asked.

"The cleaner's, of course!" Andy cried, running to his bike.

"Sorry," Mr. Martin said. "No Championship rings. Will that be cash or charge?" He held up a clear plastic package with the dark jacket inside.

"No," Seth said. "Mr. Joyner'll pick it up later. He just sent us here to check out the pocket."

Rachel looked up into the huge blue neon sign that said, "Martin's 24-Hour Cleaners."

"You're sure about this," Andy said to Mr. Martin. "No rings of any kind in the pocket?"

"Positive," Mr. Martin said. "Would you like to check the pocket yourself?" He held up the package.

"No, that won't be necessary," Andy said sadly. "C'mon. Let's get out of here."

The four friends walked glumly to their bikes and headed back to Bloom Field. H.P. rode in the basket of Rachel's bike.

"Now I've got to go back there and tell my mom and Ms. Pollack that I lost the ring," Andy said.

"What'll your mom do to you?" Seth asked.

"It's not what my mom will do to me. It's how disappointed she'll be. She was really proud that I was old enough to have that ring. And now look what I've done."

When they reached the field, Andy got off his bike and slowly began to walk over to where his mother and

Ms. Pollack were having coffee. The other three Sluggers leaned against the fence and watched.

"Hey, Rachel," Zach said. "Isn't there anything we can do? I've never seen Andy look so blue before."

Rachel shrugged her shoulders, lost in thought. "What'd you say, Zach?"

"I said, I've never seen Andy look so blue before," Zach repeated.

Suddenly Zach saw "the look" crossing Rachel's face.

"What?" he cried. "What is it, Rach? Spill it quick, before Andy gets to his mom!"

"The trouble is," Rachel said, "I'm not sure of it. I'd like to check something out before I —"

"There's no time!" Zach yelled. "Do you have an idea or *not*?"

Rachel threw up her hands. "Quick," she said, "run and get Andy and tell him to come back!"

Andy seemed annoyed when he returned.

"This better be good," he said. "I just worked up the nerve to tell my mom. I don't know if I can do it twice in one day."

"Is Mr. Joyner still there?" Rachel asked.

"He'll be umpiring the next game," Andy said. "Why?"

"Go ask him if he'll open the trunk of his car for us," Rachel said.

"His *car trunk*?" Andy cried. "What for?"

"Just do it," Rachel said. "Tell him we need to look for something in his trunk."

Andy gave Rachel a look. "You sure of this, Rachel?"

"I'm not answering that question, Andy," she said. "Just go and get the ump!"

Five minutes later, they were standing next to a green sedan in the parking lot.

"Would you open the trunk, Mr. Joyner?" Rachel asked.

The umpire stuck in the key. The latch turned and the big trunk door popped up. Inside was his old spare umpire's jacket. Except it didn't look so old.

"Check out the label," Rachel said.

"Hey," Seth cried. "This isn't the right jacket. It's got a *white* label instead of a blue one!"

"Can we look inside the pocket?" Rachel asked Mr. Joyner.

"Go ahead," said the umpire, looking at Andy.

Andy reached inside and pulled something out. It was small and metal. It had a large red stone in the center and the date 1954 on the side.

"The *ring*!" all of them cried.

"I can't believe it!" Andy roared, jumping for joy. "How did you . . . I mean what did you . . ."

"No time now," Rachel said. "Get back over to your mom, quick!"

In the Southside Ice Cream Shop the next morning, the four friends sat huddled over the *Lotus Times*. It was open to Section B. There was a big color picture of Andy and Grandpa Ike's Championship ring.

"I still can't believe how you solved this thing," Andy said. "I mean, what was the clue?"

"When Zach said Andy looked *blue*," Rachel said. "That reminded me of that bright *blue* neon light at Martin's Cleaners."

"And how did that figure in?" Andy asked.

"Well," Rachel said. "It was dark when Mr. Joyner got to the cleaner's. He had two jackets in his trunk— the old one with the blue label, and the long-sleeved one with the white label. He was supposed to drop off the long-sleeved jacket with the white label. So I thought to myself, *In* blue *light, what color would a* white *label look?*

"Blue," Zach said.

"And what color would a *blue* light make a *blue* label look?" Rachel asked.

"White," Seth said.

"Are you sure?" Andy asked.

Rachel nodded and pointed to Andy's ring.

"She's right," Seth said. "In blue light, white looks blue—and blue looks white. Mr. Joyner must've dropped off the old jacket with the blue label. That's why we didn't find the ring in his pocket."

"Let me get this straight," Andy said. "He thought the blue label was white so he dropped off the older jacket instead of the long-sleeved jacket?"

"Exactly," Rachel said. "Amazing, isn't it?"

Zach asked Andy if he could look at his ring for a minute. Andy handed it to him.

"Hey, I finally figured out what 'swing from the heart' means," Zach said, after inspecting the ring.

"What?" Seth said.

Zach took a piece of string from his pocket and threaded it through the ring. Then he tied the string around Andy's neck. The ring swung down over Andy's heart like a necklace.

"Get it?" Zach asked, with a broad smile. "Swing from the heart?"

"Very funny!" Andy laughed. "Very funny!"

Coach Terwilliger's Corner

Hi, there, all you Sluggers!

Would you like to know more about championship rings? In fact, let's talk about the most important of all championship rings—the World Series rings of Major League baseball.

First of all, they're very expensive! Even a recent World Series ring—belonging to a lesser-known player—can cost $5,000.

Since the 1920s, every player on a World Series championship team has been given a ring. These World series rings are considered the biggest prizes in baseball. Most players wouldn't give up their Championship rings for anything in the world.

But World Series winners aren't the only ones to get rings. Teams that lose a series can also wind up with World Series rings. It's up to the owners of the losing teams to decide whether or not their players will get World Series rings.

On rare occasions, some rings do fall into the hands

of collectors. Probably the most famous ring known to be sold was a Lou Gehrig ring. It was purchased in the late 1920s for a reported $8,000. The same ring would be at least four times as valuable today.

Who has the most rings? Probably the great Hall of Fame catcher Yogi Berra. He played on fourteen pennant winners with the New York Yankees. And if you add in Yogi's All-Star rings, he has enough baseball jewelry to cover all his fingers and toes!

Which rings are the best? Well, that depends on who you ask. Generally, rings presented to the winning team are more valuable than those given to the losers. And famous players' rings are more in demand than rings that belonged to ordinary players.

As far as looks go, the 1977 Yankee Championship ring—with "NY" spelled out in diamonds—is at the top of the list.

One word of warning. Rings are also given out to nonplayers who work for teams. There's only one way to know for sure if a World Series ring belonged to a certain player. Check to see what name is engraved on the back of the ring.

That's all for now. See you in the next Southside Sluggers Baseball Mystery. Until then, Play ball!

Coach Terwilliger